Sezan Mahmud is a Bangladeshi-American writer, lyricist, screenwriter, columnist, and Harvard-trained academic in public health and medicine. He has published, so far, thirty books in his mother tongue, Bengali, in wide genres, namely psychoanalytic-magic-realism, docu-novel, science fiction, and children's literature. He has received a national academy award in literature from Bangladesh. His stories were retold in movies, translated into English, and included in the National Curriculum and Textbook Board of Bangladesh. His ethnographic documentary film, *The Morgue,* has received recognition from the Richmond International Film Festival. He has published more than fifty scientific and academic articles, book chapters under his official name, Dr. Saleh M. M. Rahman.

Books by Sezan Mahmud (Selected):

1. ***Operation Jackpot*** – A docu-novel based on the true and untold story of the Naval Commando Operation in the liberation war of Bangladesh in 1971.
2. ***Haram O Onnyano Galpo*** – Collection of short stories. (Published in Bengali)
3. ***Science Fiction Samagra, Vol.1*** – A compilation of four science fiction novellas. (Published in Bengali)
4. ***Harvard er Smriti O Onny ek America*** – Memoir at the Harvard University and America. (Published in Bengali)
5. ***MuktiJuddher Kishor Rachana Samogra, Vol.1*** – A compilation of four novels/docu-novels based on the liberation war of Bangladesh. (Published in Bengali)
6. ***Path Haranor Path, Vol.1*** – A compilation of published columns. (Published in Bengali)
7. ***Science Based Adventure Samagra, Vol.1*** – A compilation of four science-based adventure novellas. (Published in Bengali)
8. ***Chhoray Chhoray Science Fiction*** – Collection of science fiction rhymes. (Published in Bengali)
9. ***Habijabi*** – Collection of juvenile rhymes. (Published in Bengali)
10. ***Palte Shudhu Lebas*** – Collection of political rhymes. (Published in Bengali)

This book is dedicated to my wife, Trishna, and my sons, Tishian Mahmud (Athoy) and Renoa Mahmud (Prem), for their sacrifices for me so that I can keep writing.

Sezan Mahmud

FIRE BORN

Translated by:
Dr. Fayeza Hasanat

AUSTIN MACAULEY PUBLISHERS™
LONDON • CAMBRIDGE • NEW YORK • SHARJAH

Ordering Information:
Quantity sales: special discounts are available on quantity purchases by corporations, associations, and others. For details, contact the publisher at the address below.

Publisher's Cataloging-in-Publication data
Mahmud, Sezan
Fire Born

ISBN 9781641829717 (Paperback)
ISBN 9781641829724 (Hardback)
ISBN 9781645366553 (ePub e-book)

Library of Congress Control Number: 2020901823

www.austinmacauley.com/us

First Published (2020)
Austin Macauley Publishers LLC
40 Wall Street, 28th Floor
New York, NY 10005
USA

mail-usa@austinmacauley.com
+1 (646) 5125767

20200916

Acknowledgement

My original publisher, Mofidul Haque of Sahittya Prokash, for his permission to publish; translator, Dr. Fayeza Hasanat, for her time and permission to publish; and my copy editor.

"It's enough for me to be sure that you and I exist at this moment."

— <u>Gabriel García Márquez,</u>

Chapter 1

The Beginning Marks the End

"Hey-ho! Watch out, Brother, be on your guard!" Boatman Gauri's high-pitched voice surpassed the gushing wind, the cascading rain, and the clamorous river. Words of caution vibrated like bellowing waves. Rain-drenched, he was standing by the riverbank. Sharp arrows of raindrops pierced the uncovered parts of his body: his face. Misty curtains of the incessant downpour blurred the distant village from his vision. Amidst the ceaseless water and the blustery wind, Gauri's little boat was only an inept necessity. With his strong muscular arm, Gauri sculled through the restless river, battling every wave with utmost mastery and yelling at the top of his voice, "Hey-ho! Watch out, Brother, be on your guard!"

The moment the boat reached near the shore, Gauri raised his oar and pushed it toward him. He spread his hands and tried to grab the oar. The flat end of the long wooden shaft slipped from his wind-struck and rain-soaked hands. Soft mud crept inside his toenails that desperately clutched the shifting ground beneath; his body gave up balance and was just a slant away from plummeting into the darkness of the turbulent river. Boatman Gauri screamed again, "Hey-ho! Watch out, Brother, be on your guard!"

Helaluddin woke up to find himself stuck in the graying dunes between dream and reality. He could hear the heavy thud of a hammer in his heart and feel the stream of sweat pouring through his skin. Someone knocked. He lifted up his head a little and threw a confused glance at the locked door that was rhythmically thudding. He could not remember what time it was, or why he locked the door and went for a nap. *Must be Asya*, he thought. No one else had the courage to disturb him when he slept, not even Helena, especially in her current condition. Extremely irritated by the housemaid's constant banging on the door Helaluddin got up and opened the door, to find Asya's face smeared with a frightened look.

"What is wrong?" Helaluddin almost screamed, even though he already knew the answer.

"Ghota Mian is here to talk to you. There's been a fight at Sonai Isle."

"Oh, okay," he said nonchalantly and went back inside. He could clearly hear the racketing crowd from his room.

It was a feud over this island that had been under his possession for a long time. In fact, he'd rather call it an attempt to rob him off of his legitimate possession. Helaluddin's security guards had already informed him of this imminent upheaval. Tota, the leader of his security team, kept all the guards prepared to tackle any upcoming trouble. Earlier this morning, Helaluddin had spent a few hours with Tota and his sentries to finalize their preparations for a possible attack. He'd not get involved in a direct fight; he'd rather orchestrate the game from behind the curtains. Helaluddin specifically ordered them to avoid the mayhem of bloodshed by all means. He had full confidence in Tota and his gang, and yet he was apprehensive when he came home after the meeting this morning and decided to take a nap to refresh his mind. He sometimes did that, falling asleep while confounding with troubles and anxieties. Was it a protective mechanism of his brain? He did not know. He only knew he needed these catnaps that gave back his mind its usual agility as it did just now. He was asleep and dreaming. But why the same dream, again and again? This was the third time he had the dream. The incident was engraved on his head in such lucid detail, like one of those haunting moments of reality, that he did not consider it a dream anymore. It felt like a flashback, with Boatman, Gauri, trying to enact a scene from his past. In a village by a river, where Helaluddin spent his childhood days, there really lived a boatman named Gauri. But why was Gauri trying to warn him? How grave was the danger? What horrifying presentiments ushered Gauri back from a past and persuaded him to stalk Helaluddin's dreams, rowing a tiny dinghy on a turbulent river in a stormy night and sending a cry of caution at his direction? Helaluddin's eyes wandered through the window, in an attempt to see the unforeseen and decipher the meanings of the commotion that was forming, somewhere out there, on his island.

The road that brought Helaluddin to this home-island was tainted in every step with uncertainty and anguish, fear and thrill. Many times, island seekers like him had tried to take control of his land by force. But Helaluddin never gave in, nor did he invade any island claimed or marked by others. He walked mile after mile on foot, rowed his boat from river to river, only in search of some claimable, habitable islands. Some were far away, and some, totally uncultivable. But no obstacle stopped him from searching for new lands where he hoped to build a new society within the periphery of the existing one. Was that a feasible hope that he had, or was it just an empty pursuit of an impossible dream? Was he just a mirage chaser? How long would this arid chase of his continue? Where would it end and when? What was the point if, at the end of the game, the only remaining thing would be nothing but his broken, fatigued shadow? The crowd grew louder outside as Helaluddin started sinking deep into this unfathomable ocean of unanswerable questions. But a life without a search for the unknowable was meaningless for him. A life without the angst of excitement was utterly vain. It was this boundless yearning for the quest, this passionate longing for adventure that always made him feel alive.

"There is something in you, I like more than yourself. Therefore I must destroy you."

— <u>Jacques Lacan</u>

Chapter 2

Feud Sparks in Isle Sonai

Noor Mohammad was not a devout Muslim. He was not even regular in following the daily prayer rituals. Waking up every morning at dawn and dragging his body to the mosque was a tedious task. But he still did it just to avoid being reprimanded by the villagers, his tutor at the Madrassa and sometimes, by his conscience. That morning, after coming back from Fajr prayer at the mosque, he was trying to get back to his sleep cycle when Asya started knocking at his door.

"Wake up, wake up, there's been a feud over the possession of Isle Sonai! Wake up! This is not the time for you to stay in bed!"

Noor Mohammad startled and sat up. Asya's knocking had awakened him from a nightmare that was still beating like a hammer in his heart. He was never comfortable with these terms: feud, fight, contest, and chaos—over a piece of land. Now people would run around, with weapons in their hands, shrieking for each other's blood; and then there would be bloodshed, crying, mourning, police, and arrest. Noor Mohammad never physically witnessed these fighting sprees; Uncle Helaluddin always protected him from any such exposure and the dangers that lay in its path. Though he never saw how they ran the combat, Noor Mohammad had seen Tota Mian's extensive preparation throughout the year for any incumbent fight. Tota Mian was the leader of Uncle Helaluddin's *lathial* troop. He was in charge of recruiting strong men and training them to become invincible masters of fighting with *lathi*—the strong and sturdy bamboo-staff. He would select and cut strong and mature culms of timber bamboo, polish them constantly with oil until they were ready to be used as martial art weapons. He would appoint the village blacksmith to forge spears, swords, thatched bamboo, shields, axes, short and longbows, machetes, long bamboo poles with sharp metal blades; Tota Mian knew how to prepare all his weapons and his men to take care of anyone who tried to seize any part of any island owned by Uncle Helaluddin. His uncle was feared by opponents for his strength and respected by the villagers for his kindness. The poor landless farmers were grateful to him for letting them survive on this remote island by the Yamuna River. After claiming the island, Uncle had built homes for the poor, primary schools for the children, a madrassa for religious education. He had built a mosque and a deep tube well. He was a strong and cruel man with a soft heart, people said, like those kings of the old days. But this cruel man was never anything but kind and loving toward him.

Noor Mohammad came outside. He could hear the wind rustling through the oval leaves of the big jackfruit tree from the left side of the house; and he could hear people, screaming and shouting somewhere. Someone wanted to take away this island from them, and the fight had already started! The very thought of such bout numbed his head; a blunt pain started to erupt through his veins, throbbing and swirling inside his skull. Oh, the painful sound of a roaring wind! Just like the one he had heard the day he went to see Isle Sonai for the first time. It was early morning. The emerging rays of the rising sun fell on the sands, making each sand speck sparkle like gold. The sparkling light also glowed at the corners of Uncle Rahimuddin's eyes. Noor Mohammad was spellbound! He was striding over the body of a newly formed land of golden sand. The morning wind was dancing all around and the shiny sand specks were dancing with it. The playful wind was whishing into the glowing sand and gushing out, soughing, like an endless aerial song. Noor Mohammad sat down on the wet sand and grabbed a handful of golden specks.

"Look, Uncle, look!" He screamed, "Look at this golden sand! You should call this one an island of gold! Name it Isle Sonai."

"That's a nice name! Isle Sonai!" Uncle sounded pleased.

Once they came back from the island, Uncle Helaluddin asked his drummer to announce the name of his newfound island. The drummer walked around the village announcing the birth of a new island that had just been claimed by Helaluddin.

Isle Sonai was separated from their village by a big lake. The lake also eventually came to be known as Lake Sonai. And the beautiful golden sand of that beautiful island would be drenched in blood today. Bloodthirsty fighters were gathering on that island just to brand it with a proprietorial claim. The wind that lashed through the oval leaves of the big Jackfruit tree rushed into his head, howling and moaning, piercing through him towards the locked door at his left, wherein lay a woman, who was banging her shackles on the floor and groaning like a caged animal. As the russet sands of Isle Sonai blew inside his head, the soughing wind and the groaning voice pierced him like blunt blades of darkening pain, Noor Mohammad started to run away from everything audible.

"How hard it is to become a man again when one has ceased to be a man."

— <u>*Alejo Carpentier*</u>

Chapter 3
Reflection in the Shadows of Water

The dead silence of this side of the island was only violated by occasional appearances of a few birds; kingfishers, storks, cranes, emerging from the perennial groves of *Kans* grass, flapping their wings. By now, Noor Mohammad had mastered how to keep his focus amidst the commotion. Uncle Helaluddin kept a tiny boat by the bank, with its oars hidden under the deck. Whenever the sounds of silence roared inside his head, Noor Mohammad would run to this side of the bank, untie his dinghy and jump in, rowing it to the middle of the river, letting it afloat, while he sat in the middle of the boat in a prayer posture, with legs folded, eyes closed, and his body, erect and yet surrendered. And that was his moment to feel the tranquility. His mind became lighter than feathers, and the white wild sugarcane bloom. He could see through his mind's eye the swinging little wooden boat, circling in the middle of the river, absorbing sounds and sights. Everything around him gradually faded away, like a horizontal bar of stillness, as he sat with his knees bent and his palms placed on them, reciting the Quran from his memory. He could recite every verse without faltering: from *Surah Fatiha to Surah Naas*. Moulavi, the head cleric of the Madrassa, was always amazed to hear, Noor Mohammad, recite the Quran from his memory so flawlessly. He never saw anyone who memorized the whole Quran at such a tender age. To him, Noor Mohammad was a miracle from Allah. Noor Mohammad, however, did not think it was too hard of a job. He only had to read it twice to have it memorized! And since then, anytime he came across an internal crisis, he would come to sit here in the middle of the river and recite every verse until his sores healed. He would do it clockwise, and everything would happen accordingly: the birds would flap away a silent river and his mind would clear all the clutters inside him, around him, until solitude deafened him. He sat in his prayer position, waiting for the deafening silence, but always felt interrupted by something. A feeling of a presence. From the distant horizon of stillness came a stranger's voice, talking to him, calling him, breaking his meditation. Should he open his eyes? Should he go away? Should he follow the voice and find its source? Should he call out for help, or share this experience with someone? But to what use? Who would understand the turmoil that lies beneath a river's calm? He rather accepted that uncanny voice of a shapeless being as his inevitable companion, like the boat and the river, and the thick forest of wild sugarcane by the bank of the river.

This morning, he sat on his boat, with his eyes closed, accompanied by a roaring wind storm stuck in his head and anticipating every moment, a stranger's voice rasping around him, and he thought he finally heard him:

"Brother Noor!"

He opened his eyes as the voice called again.

"Brother Noor!"

It was Ghota Mian, Uncle Helaluddin's ward, standing by the bank, like a quivering shadow blocking the morning sun.

"Brother Noor, Mr. Talukdar is hunting for you!"

Ghota Mian's limited dialect confused one verb with another. For him, hunting and looking for someone was the same thing. If you do not find someone or anything, you hunt for it, until you find what you are looking for, right?

"Is the fight over?" Noor Mohammad asked.

"Long time ago!" Tota Mian's fighter team beat the contenders easily!"

"Anyone died? Is the police here?"

"Nah, no one died. Some just got injured." Ghota sounded disappointed that the fight ended without much gore.

Noor Mohammad rowed back to the shore and tied his boat.

"Go ahead, Ghota Mian. I'll follow."

He sat on the corner and kept looking at the water, at his own reflection. He drooped down, keeping his stare fixed on the image, floating in the calm water surface. He could see his face, and the blue sky behind it, and the white morning cloud floating in the sky dipped in water. He saw his face shake and tremble, quiver, and grow. He suddenly realized how his face had grown. The image shifted its shape and reflected a face that was not his own, but he knew its owner. He kept looking at the crystal-clear water of the river and saw Uncle Helaluddin's face staring back at him, with the same face. Every time he came to this river for meditation and sat to catch his own reflection in the river, he only saw Uncle's face, looking at him, just the way it was staring back, right now.

"Are you coming?" Ghota Mian shouted from a distance. "Don't be late!"

As Noor Mohammad stepped down from the boat, the idle water lost its calm and the reflection dismembered into a multitude of ripples.

"Rise and demand; you are a burning flame. You are sure to conquer there where the final horizon Becomes a drop of blood, a drop of life, Where you will carry the universe on your shoulders, Where the universe will bear your hope."

– *Miguel Angel Asturias*

Chapter 4

Beware of a Rising Threat

Man is an ungrateful beast. Like the hungry pigs in a sty, the ruthless cattle on a ranch, the lowest breed of stray dogs, man is the unruly animal in this brutal jungle in which, the mere survival for struggle is a nightmare. He had seen it all: from the days of the useless existence to the rising days of power in a man's life. He was nothing, but a pretentious thug to others during those struggling days. They slighted him, called him names: Helal the-wanna-be thug, Hostile Helal, or Helailla until he managed to buy the chunk of land from Babu Susilkanta, in Shohugpur. The possession of land gave him the status of a Talukdar, the owner of the enviable amount of land property. But this land-laid aristocracy came with its own curse. There would be fights over possession of newly risen islands and after every fight, there would be the endless racket: treat the wounded, bury the dead, handle the police, manage lawyers, file lawsuit and get sued; he managed to complete everything on his own, with meticulous skill, and yet failed to please those brutes. Helaluddin took out the bowl from his hookah and tapped it on the ground, to shake off the remnants of burnt-out tobacco leaves. For a moment, the coconut shell of a hookah bowl transformed itself into the lump of ungrateful mankind and took a thrashing on its behalf. After shaking and tapping it for a few long minutes, Helaluddin, refilled the hookah bowl with freshly dried tobacco leaves that were hand-picked for him, from his own field and then, fermented in thick molasses. He took a good number of puffs, long and relaxing ones, and dazed, waiting for the vaporized tobacco to start working its miracle.

This was a dangerous time for anyone to approach Helaluddin, anyone, except Noor Mohammad.

"Did you want to see me, Uncle?"

"Yes. Where have you been?" Helaluddin knew the answer but he still asked. He always found Noor Mohammad's dinghy, stalling in the mid-river a bit unnerving. His experience with Helena had taught him to be apprehensive of such unusual activities.

"Went to the river; stalled the boat in mid-river."

"Okay. At least you stayed away from the uproar." Helaluddin said as he pulled his nephew closer. "Let's go see your mother. She's not feeling well." Two of them walked together to her room across the yard.

A middle-aged woman lay on the floor, shackled. Her hands and feet were tied with a long chain, secured tightly with a pillar at the left corner of the room. Her eyes looked blurry, like the murky river of a rainy season. Two fading water lines ran from the corners of her eyes, drying halfway near her ears, as reminders of remnant rains.

"How are you feeling, Helena?" Helaluddin asked.

"Ma!" Noor Mohammad softly whispered.

The soft whisper ushered a flow of tears that gushed like raindrops from two blurry eyes, washing off the vacant look. Helaluddin knew it was time to unchain her. He took the padlock out of the shackles and freed her hands and feet. Helena sat up as if nothing ever went wrong and pulled her son to her bosom. There was no sign of the irrational craze in her anymore. Even she would not believe it, had anyone told her that she chased Ghota Mian this morning, and tried to kill him with a fish-cutting knife. The mother in her was awake and wanted to love her child, feed him and take care of him to her best ability.

"Did you have your lunch, dear?"

"No, Ma."

"Okay, let's go to the kitchen. I will feed you with my own hand. Let me see if there's any Hilsa fish curry left."

People said his mother was crazy. They did not say anything in front of him, because they could not. They were always afraid of Uncle Helal. But Noor Mohammad knew they spoke of her as a lunatic, and maybe more. But when his mother had control over her head, like right now, she told him stories and taught him things. Noor Mohammad knew how easily she could become the best mother for him, and the best teacher.

Helena brought a plate full of rice and Hilsa fish curry for her son. She ran her fingers through the white jasmine rice to mix it well with the curry, before taking out the bones from the fish and making little lumps of rice and fish. Like a statue, Helaluddin sat motionlessly and watched the mother and her son.

It took him a few days to restore normalcy in the village after the isle bout. Once life went back to resume its normal cycle, Helaluddin decided to dig deep into the matter. Yes, his people were able to keep control and defeat the opposition, but who was the ringleader? Who was provoking those villagers to team up and fight against his valid ownership? Who was it that ignited this useless rebellion? Helaluddin appointed Surat Ali, to work for him as a spy, asking him to mingle with the crowd on weekly market days and gather information. Surat Ali was a clever young man; he knew how to talk and what to look for. He knew all he had to do was sit by the tea stall of the marketplace and ask irrelevant questions. The truth would eventually unfold. Helaluddin knew that it would be a matter of a few weeks before Surat Ali would come back with the information. But he was more concerned about the timing of the threat. Why now? Why was someone trying to topple his authority at a time when the whole country was just on the verge of imminent danger? He had to know more about the upcoming troubles looming on the horizon of his island, his country.

Noor Mohammad's learning process was divided into two phases: he learned his Islamic education from the village Madrassa, and his Bengali and English from Pundit Khagen, a Hindu barber by profession, but a devout house tutor by passion. Pundit Khagen had tutored a good number of Hindu students of wealthy families in town. Helaluddin had appointed him to teach Noor Mohammad how to read and write, in both Bengali and English. Every morning the master and his pupil sat under the big Jackfruit tree, where the master taught an inquisitive learner, everything he could: A book of the Bengali Alphabet by Ishwar Chandra Vidyasagar, Book of Arithmetic by Jadav. The pupil was instructed to improve his handwriting by practicing on a big banana leaf instead of writing on a chalkboard. The little pupil also learned, each Bengali alphabet and word: simple and compound word structure, and then gradually started reading alphabet rhymes:

If you break the bed, then bed on the ground.
The fruit is fragrant when full-grown.
Never tell a lie. Never quarrel with anyone. Never curse. Never disobey your parents and never be unruly. Do not run in the sun. Do not make a noise when someone is studying. Do not play all day long. Gopal is a good boy and listens to his parents. Gopal always does his homework and never quarrels with anyone. He obeys his teachers and loves his siblings. He helps his parents. He does not play on his way to or back from school. When he goes home, he takes a shower and eats whatever food his mother offers; then he completes his homework before going out to play. Gopal does not give anyone any trouble. He loves all and is loved by all. Every boy should be like Gopal.

Helaluddin always sat beside the teacher and his pupil during these lessons. He loved listening to Noor Mohammad's rendition every morning, be it from Vidyasagar's rapid reader or Allah's Quran. An inexplicable electric spark ran through his veins as he sat there every morning, listening to Noor Mohammad's melodious voice. At times it sparked pleasures of pride, and at times, it was that chilling knife of fear that cut through him inside, leaving the gaping wounds of unspoken secrets in open display. Why did he run after the excitement of island hunting? Was it because he wanted to run away from the reach of a haunting past, or was it because, he was desperate to create an alternate new world, that was free from the marks of isolation and rejections? Was Island Sonai, his dream vision of a guilt-free world?

Pundit Khagen came from Rajapur, a village quite far away. But the distance was not an issue for this enthused teacher, who walked about four miles and take a ferry every day, only to teach Noor Mohammad. Never late, never missed a day, until today. Helaluddin's forehead wrinkled in apprehension. He sent Ghota Mian to Rajapur, to find out what made the Pundit break his routine.

In the evenings, Helaluddin sat among his farming laborers, sharing a conversation, and puffing tobacco from a hookah. These were his seasonal workers, who came from different places and worked for food and nominal wage. After a day's hard work, these migrant workers sat together in the outer room, eating food and smoking bidi and hookah. Shredded dried tobacco neatly rolled in dried tobacco leaves, bidi as they called it, was the secret attraction of these gatherings. Helaluddin enjoyed how these people laughed over simple things and fought for a puff of a slim bidi. Surat Ali came back from the town and asked him for a private meeting. He brought news.

"Rumor says Mojnu Mian is behind all this," he said.

"Which one? Mojnu from the village Betil or the one from Nishi Boyra?"

"Betil."

"Are you sure?"

"Positive. Everyone in the Bazaar was saying so. Besides, Mojnu himself was there, racketing about how he would avenge the assault that your people inflicted on his gang."

"How did he get this powerful? How come he is he suddenly so brave and mighty?"

"Got flow of money, I think. Just established a paddy husking mill and a brickwork, you know."

"Yes, but that's not the main source of his power."

"What is, then?"

"Chora Matin."

"Who?"

"Abdul Matin, that corrupted man from Muslim League, remember? Mojnu Mian recently became his follower, a new disciple."

Surat Ali became worried. When did all this happen, and most importantly, how did Helaluddin know? He tried as hard as he could, to look directly into Helaluddin's eyes and see some hint of light, that would give him some direction toward the real truth, in such a dark night.

"God waits to win back his own flowers as gifts from man's hands."

– <u>Rabindranath Tagore</u>

Chapter 5
Flames of Fire God

Pundit Khagen came the next day. With his head shaved and his lean body wrapped in one piece of cotton, he was hardly recognizable. His father had passed away, the Pundit informed, and he had to shave his head to perform his funeral ritual as a son. He was not supposed to come out of his house, but at times mere financial needs superseded religious customs. He was following the rest of the ritual, though: eating only rice and vegetables, one meal every day. As usual, Noor Mohammad bent down to touch the Pundit's feet; it was his uncle's order that he took every teacher's blessing the same way, irrespective of their religion. Pundit Khagen gave Noor Mohammad his blessing and sat down to start the day's lesson. But something was off. The Pundit was not himself; his mind was wandering away, his lessons were becoming incongruent, and his disinterested attitude became explicit even to the young learner sitting in front of him.

"Punditjee, you seem to be unwell today. It is okay if you do not wish to continue today's lesson," Noor Mohammad politely said. He took extra caution in selecting the right words in his speech; the pundit never liked to hear dialects or slangs. "Language needs to be clear and correct. Words should be rich and sophisticated; after all, they are the ones that give you meaning," the pundit always said. Uncle Helal also said the same thing: "your words tell others who you are, so make a careful selection of words, images. When you are reading the Quran, recite every word correctly and perfect your pronunciation of Arabic; do the same when you are speaking in Bangla. It is a pure language too, and does deserve your equal devotion." Pundit Khagen was the only person with whom Noor Mohammad could speak in perfect Bangla. People in his village and all around him only spoke in dialects. The Moulavi, of the Madrassa, was displeased when he found out that; Helaluddin Talukdar had hired a Hindu teacher for his nephew's non-Islamic education.

"Why, Mister Talukdar? You don't think we'd be good teachers for him! We can teach Bangla and Mathematics. We can; can't we?" The Moulavi once complained.

"Don't make a fuss over it, Moulavi!" Uncle Helaluddin retorted, "You do what you are good at and let him do what he does best; besides, Hindus make a good teacher, way better than you people are."

The Moulavi never said anything after that.

"Sir, really, it is alright if you are not in the mood to teach today."

"Okay. I am not in the mood you are right, but I can tell you stories if you want to hear."

"Yes, I want to hear your stories. Tell me about gods and goddesses. Tell me how you deal with so many deities?

"We only have one God and you have so many!"

"Well, it doesn't matter how many you have; they all round-up as one. It is just that; Hinduism is a quite ancient religion that follows the rituals that had been with it since antiquity."

The Pundit looked away, with a distant look in his eyes, and kept muttering about millions of gods and goddesses and their harmonious integration. "Let's say, fire: Fire the God of all gods It's not only the fire that you see; it is what you can't see. It is what runs beneath all creation; it is the real feature of Mother Earth. You see lightning, and you see the starts and the sun. All are just orbs and lines of fire. Fire. God of gods. It hides in the sap of trees, in woods and rocks, in clouds; it ignites from rubbing two things—just the way the caveman first realized—by rubbing and chafing two rock-solid elements, he had his first meeting with this god. The Caveman saw the light of the fire, and a god was born. But what is this God like? What is its shape? Its color? Music has seven tunes, a rainbow has seven colors, and fire has its seven flames. Seven flames from whence are born forty-nine types of fire. The Fire God with its seven scorching tongues: eats up and burns up everything, leaving behind mounds of ashes, purifying the whole world with his light and warmth, while burning and devouring everything that falls in front of him—this Fire God!"

Like a Chorus in a Morality play, the Pundit delivered, nonstop, an eloquent piece. His fiery words flew around Noor Mohammad, like invisible flames, and felt his heart with warmth—the kind of warmth that he usually felt after reciting a few verses from the Quran.

Pundit Khagen was really upset that morning. He told Noor Mohammad about his deceased father. Pundit

Khagen's father died unhappy. After the partition, most of the people from Rajapur had left for West Bengal, but his father refused to go. He did not want to leave his own home, his heritage, his memories behind, and create a new home somewhere else. Rajapur was his home, his root. "He would rather die here," he used to say. Pundit Khagen's father died in his own land, but he lived an unhappy life. He saw the sufferings of his Hindu neighbors and how one group of neighbors robbed another group of their lands and properties just because they were of a different religion. He had seen how Montaz Shekh's seven sons took away the lands that belonged to the Shaha family. Shaha's younger son, Babu, went stark mad after losing everything. He became a homeless beggar and lived on other's pity. People now called him Crazy Babu. Pundit Khagen wiped his eyes in his shirtsleeve and got up, leaving Noor Mohammad stuck in a cage of painful memories. Noor Mohammad remembered the pain he saw in Bindubashini's eyes the other day. Bindubashini, once a rich Hindu wife and widow, is now a mere beggar, living with her two daughters in the house that she and her late husband, had shared for so many years. "She only had the house," she had told Uncle Helal; the rest of her property had been taken away by the powerful men of her village. She and her two daughters survived by working as maids: husking paddy, puffing rice, or by selling fresh produce from their garden. Bindubashini always brought a big basket whenever she came to see uncle: the best kind of Chira-puffed rice, and fruit from her orchard— mangoes, pomegranates, bananas. She knew Uncle Helal would pay her well. She had burnt her good days in the funeral pyre of her husband and bracing each of her adverse says with a nonchalant attitude; she had nothing else to lose, besides her two daughters. And she was constantly afraid of losing them, sacrificing them to the hungry hyenas of the village. Montaz Shekh's son was after one of her daughters and was always threatening to abduct her. Uncle Helal had tried to make peace between them, but it was of no avail. No one could save her two girls from these predators, she knew. And so did Noor Mohammad; hearing to Pundit Khagen's lamentation this morning and reminiscing Bindubashini's tales of sufferings, Noor Mohammad felt a pang, a sudden surge of an emotion that was unbeknownst to him, and felt himself being drawn into the center of that chasm, submerged and then spewed out into this overwhelming flow of despondent mature life. Was he really growing up? That fast? Noor Mohammad left his books in his room and ran outside. He needed to breathe fresh air. The Afternoon was glowing everywhere: on the tin roofs of houses, over the sandy fields, in the leaves of *Jiga* trees that stood in line by the roadside and at every backyard. The gluey sap from these trees worked as a perfect binding agent for the cutting line of a kite. Kite-fighters always polished their cutting lines with the paste of powdered glass and sap from the *Jiga* tree. This glass-coated line would be a powerful tool for kite tangling, especially with *Chila* kites. But Noor Mohammad preferred *Koira guddi* the most. A scarp piece of cheap construction paper tied down around two thin wicker sticks that are bent and polished to give the kite a diamond shape, dived up in the air with the support of a pair of triangular tales that larked beneath and hung like swiveling propellers. The *Koira guddi* that Ghota Mian had made for him last year was still the largest one in the village. He remembered the pride he felt last year, around this time when Ghota Mian handed him the spool. He launched the big kite into the air and kept control, tugging the line at times, and at times, letting out the line, allowing a piece of paper and a bow of two wicker sticks to flap and swell and fully erect, catching tinsel of endless wind in between its tail. He still had the kite in his possession, but the desire to fly it was not there anymore; he had outgrown the kite and its wind-catching dreams. His own nocturnal dreams were signaling him that Ghota Mian's kite was not enough to contain his desires anymore. It was not a good thing, he knew; the Moulavi had told him about the bad impacts of such emissions. He woke up ashamed every night, after those passionately gratifying dreams and constantly asked for Allah's forgiveness for his sinful thoughts. He was fascinated by the dreams, by the body that caused him the dreams. Long-time ago, Noor Mohammad once went to the city Movie theatre to watch a movie with Uncle Helal. He saw a life-size poster of the movie, focusing on the female lead of that movie: a big, robust female body. He did not know the heroine's name, neither did he remember the name of the cinema. The cinema just existed in his mind as a woman's voluptuous chest. The sinful pleasure started erecting in him with the mere thought of that poster. Noor Mohammad slowly started to walk toward Madrassa. He had not seen the Moulavi for a long time.

The Moulavi was nowhere to be found. Noor Mohammad went to check the Madrassa. And from there he went to his house, and then to the mosque. He walked toward the big yard by the school, hoping to meet a few of his playmates somewhere. But the field was barren, both of grass and people. As he walked by the school veranda, four of his class friends: Omar, Lablu, Kala, and Dulal, dashed out of an empty classroom and sprinted past him. Puzzled, Noor Mohammad stood there, looking at the remnants of dust that still lingered in the path after the footsteps disappeared.

"Did you see that?"

Noor Mohammad startled, as Aminur suddenly emerged and touched him by the shoulder.

"See what?" He asked.

"Them, inside the empty classroom."

"See what?" He asked again, still perplexed.

"Them, playing the flip and bend game with each other! I saw them, through the holes in the tin-walls."

Was he hearing Aminur correctly? Did Aminur really mean—that? Oh, he was really growing fast, he had grown up! Noor Mohammad felt himself slipping through the creases of his own fingers, like the sands of time that one tried to grasp in the gaping cave of one's palms. He was changing, within and outside, without anyone's knowledge. No one wanted to befriend him because he was different: a boy who had memorized the whole Quran, who could read Bangla and knew Math, who was the nephew of the powerful Talukdar. He was so different and so aloof! He was not among them, of them, or like them—those menfolk, those boys, like Aminur or Omar or Lablu or Kala, or Dulal! Noor Mohammad's heart felt the same pang, the same swelling rupture of loneliness that he experienced this morning, after hearing Pundit Khagen's tales—of struggles, insults, glory, and of power; the power of the Fire God, with its seven flames, twirled inside his head, burning his thoughts, his senses, his very sense of existence, gaping open all those wounds inside him that are only sore with unanswerable questions. It was the story of creation that always taunted him most. This world as the birthing ground of all children of Adam and Eve. Everything and everyone came in pairs. Adam and Eve. Abel and Cain and their two sisters, and then the children of Abel and Cain. Then came more; were those children of Adam and Eve's offspring the ones from the Neolithic Age who discovered the power of fire that was hidden in the stones and in dried woods? Is fire the real god of everything—from farming to civilization? What would man be without the power of fire? And the flames—the seven flaming fires—were they living being— eternal, endless, deathless existence—the beginning and the meaning of all? Then, how come the benevolent might of fire burns homes and takes away the lives of innocents? Hadn't he seen the devouring cruelty of the flames of Summer Fires? If fire destroys everything, and if man is in control of fire, then how can its power be stain-free, uncorrupted, and untouched by man's sins? O, Oh, Oooooh, these questions, these incomprehensible, inexplicable questions! Oh, the fiery pain that burnt inside! Oh, the wilted smoke, the smoldering, fuming rings of questions that jabbed his consciousness! Noor Mohammad felt a surge of soughing wind piercing inside his head like blunt blades of darkening pain.

"On sorrow floats laughter."

— <u>Günter Grass</u>

Chapter 6

Oh, the Lamenting Ashek Noor!

Mother was busy in the kitchen. She was cleaning and cutting some vegetables. Her eyes were red from the smokes of the wood burner stove as her face caught the crimson warmth of the fire. She looked so peaceful, so pretty, sitting by the fire and preparing food, with her eyes cast downward and her long tresses of black hair flowing spreading curtain of silky warmth over her back. If only, Mother was punctual about her medicines! Noor Mohammad sighed. Uncle Helal had appointed the best psychiatrist to treat his mother's condition but his mother had recently become too stubborn that sometimes she would refuse to take any medication and sometimes hide or throw them away. She would lie to Uncle Helal if he asked her about the dosage. Noor Mohammad did not understand this lying and conniving nature of his mother. She never liked to be lied to, or she never let Noor Mohammad go unpunished for telling a whimsical lie. And yet, she would lie day after day and skip her medication and eventually suffer because of the irregularity.

"Why do you lie, mother? Why don't you take your medicine?" Noor Mohammad had once asked her.

"Because the doctor is a bad person and because he has slipped poison in my medication. I will die a slow and painful death if I take those poisonous pills."

Noor Mohammad did not know what to say or how to convince a person like his mother, who had a very strong sense of perception. He knew his mother had been like this all her life and would not change for anything; she would speak the same Bengali dialect, stay the same way, defy all the rules, and create her own world of truths and lies, and would not cease giving him her unconditional love.

"Are you hungry, kiddo?"

"Hmm."

"Just wait a little bit more. My Stem Amaranth curry is almost done."

Noor Mohammad pulled up a wooden stool and sat by her. The delicious smell of Spinach curry awakened his gustatory sense, and his stomach gave a big growl. There were days his whole body felt like this—his awakened stomach. And there were days that added years to each passing minute, making him feel older and mature than the day before. Today was one of those days. Like that day when two groups fought over the possession of Isle Sonai. He thought he grew wiser that day, but this morning's experience opened for him another dimension of wisdom; in the dungeon of his mind, two creatures of darkness were engaged in eternal combat, trying to tear away layers of emotion from reason and faith. He felt the tremor of those internal combats every time the Moulavi from the *Madrassa* tried to give him confusing or questionable interpretation of some surah or some ayah from the Quran. He would have a gut feeling against Moulavi's interpretations but could not gather the courage to spew it out. Sitting by his mother in the kitchen, he heard his gut rumbling again as the combat of his internal creatures continued while his memory flashed back the stories of Fire gods. Moulavi had warned him against the Hindu religious customs and told him never to partake in any rituals that defied the monotheistic belief of Islam. It would be blasphemy to listen to their myths; it would be sacrilegious to attend any Hindu event, the Moulavi had told him. But Uncle Helal seemed to be untouched by the conservative ideas nourished by the wise Cleric. He always attended the Hindu festivals in all the neighboring villages, and Noor Mohammad enjoyed being with him traveling from temple to temple or attending nightlong musical operas arranged by the Hindu community of the village. The mere presence of his uncle gave him strange confidence; he felt protected, loved. At any given moment of crisis, he knew the only person on whom he could depend was his uncle. Noor Mohammad had never seen his father; he never could imagine what it felt like having a father around, but he was sure that a father could be no better than his uncle Helal.

"Are you done, cooking? Helena? Hurry up! I got a guest with me."

"What do you mean? Where did you find some guests at this late hour of the day?"

"She is a wandering folk singer, a *Boyati*. I met her in the Rajapur marketplace, entertaining people with her songs. I invited her here and asked her to perform a solo musical on *Ashek Noor*. We will hear her songs all night long."

It had been a while since the people of this village had enjoyed such an event.

The whole house got caught in a hurricane of exciting activities in preparation for the upcoming musical performance by the wandering singer. They brought two wooden beds. Out in the center of the yard and joined them together to form a stage. They covered them with linens and put up a canopy right above. Beddings of rice straw were placed around the stage for sitting arrangements for the general crowd, putting women on one side of the stage, and men, on the other. A few big wooden chairs were placed at the back row for honored guests and members of the household. Bright Petromax lamps placed around the stage created an illusion of a prolonged daytime. Noor Mohammad finished his dinner with rice and chicken curry, cooked with stem amaranth. He then joined the excited crowd that gathered in their yard to enjoy a musical performance. Wrapping himself in the comfort of a warm blanket, he sat down on the cushions of rice straw, waiting for the excitement to start. People from all over the village started showing up one by one. They had to finish their daily chores before managing a little time for such leisure. They would join in groups, bring their family with them, and sit on the rice straw mattresses that were spread beneath a starlit sky, around a brightly lighted stage. Even the Moulavi did not hesitate to join the group and watch a woman perform in front of hundreds of men. Why wouldn't he? After all, for the village masses, these open stage musicals were the only available form of recreation. No one wanted to be deprived of that.

The wandering ascetic's name was Karimon. Attired in a cotton sari, nicely wrapped and tucked, carrying a two-string mandolin in her right hand, she came on the stage and started her opening song:

"I start with the name of Allah and his Prophet (saw)"

Madhab Kundu, the drummer, followed her, beating with his two hands the two drumheads of his *dhol* that hung over his belly, like a hollow earthen boat. With distinct tapping, his fingers beat the rhythm of Karimon's melodious rendition that started in the name of her Lord and followed the tragic track of a woman named Ashek Noor.

There once was a farmer girl named Askek Noor whose beauty was unparalleled. One day, while working in the field, she was spotted by a pair of hungry eyes that belonged to the Zamindar of that area. The Zamindar was instantly attracted to Ashek Noor and wanted her as his companion. He ordered Ashek Noor's father to hand her over, but how could a father do that? Especially to a daughter who was already in love with another young farmer? Have you heard of the romance of Shiri-Farhad? Of Laili-Majnu? Of Chnadi Das-Rajakini? You have? Then you can imagine how heavenly this love of Ashek Noor's was, and how blissful? How can a father destroy that bliss? How can Ashek Noor desert that love and become a pleasure companion of a rich Zamindar? What can they do to be safe from a ferocious pair of powerful eyes? O, my people, they fled, Ashek Noor and her beloved, they fled into the deep forest. They fled into the remote part of a forest, and built their new home, tilled their new soil, harvested their new crops—both in the fields and inside their home. With the birth of a beautiful son, they enjoyed the ultimate bliss of their marital life. But who says bliss is a permanent condition? Aren't we all aware of misgivings and woes? Isn't there a Zamindar in her life, looming like a stormy cloud in the sky of her happy life? Zamindar's men hunted them out and reported to their master.

> *Take a listen, my audience, the fury of Hell has no end.*
> *And neither did that cruel man*
> *The Zamindar of that distant land.*
> *He ordered his men to destroy a home,*
> *And capture the man who foiled his dreams.*
> *He ordered them to snatch a mother's child*
> *To throw him in the forest, as food for the wild.*
> *A desolate wife, a mother, bereft*
> *Ashek Noor ran around in the forest*
> *She went insane, yes, she lost her mind*
> *As she searched and ran around, crying*
> *Looking for her son, her own little boy.*
> *Oh, where had they thrown away her life, her joy?*
> *Ashek Noor cried, Ashek Noor screamed!*
> *Trees trembled in her pain and shed their leaves*
> *Leaves dropped, like tears of the forest.*
> *Oh, the lamenting Ashek Noor!*
> *How much pain can her heart endure!*

The people who came from all over the village and sat on the rice straw mattresses to enjoy a musical performance under the starlit canopy of the sky empathized with a woman named Ashek Noor. Women sobbed and wept and wiped their tears. Men puffed their hookah or inhaled some smoke from their homemade bidi and blamed the smoke for watering their eyes. Noor Mohammad needed no excuse.

48

"Memory is satisfied desire."

— <u>*Carlos Fuentes*</u>

Chapter 7

The Elation of a New Kind

Helaluddin woke up a happy person the next morning, feeling the elation of a new kind. This new feeling of excitement was blended with: both love and hatred, affection and pity, sympathy and disgust, for his fellow human beings. These people—these hardworking simple and illiterate village people—he had organized for them a night of tranquil leisure last night. They had enjoyed the musical performance of Karimon and went home with a gratified soul. They had woken up to their new day today, bracing up for the same kind of struggles for survival: fierce, ungrateful, conniving men, worse than the stray dogs, crueler than the wild hogs, eating crumbs from your hand one minute and then biting your hand off the next; planning to kill you for some utilitarian reason one minute and then giving up his life to save you. What wonderfully unpredictable and unpredictably cruel creatures, these humans are! Helaluddin's heart filled up with love for these people whom he tended to like as his own children. He brought a Neem twig and chewed its one end to turn it into soft bristles to brush his teeth with. He then took a long stride toward the riverbank.

The water was separated from the land by thick morning fog. Helaluddin walked through the damp sand to reach the crack line between the fog and the water. The brink of the river was always his favorite spot. It was a center point, and a zenith too. The horizontal edge ran like life's fragile line. Life is nothing but a moment frozen on the brink. If you want to know its meaning, then simply either take a leap or step back. He had done it so many times in his life—took a few leaps many times and recoiled from it even more.

He spread a towel on a grassy spot and sat down to watch the river current. The waves had a rhythmic melody, quite docile and definitely pleasing to watch. Yet, the same river would change its nature in the rainy seasons when it would become vicious, tearing and ripping off anything that fell in its way—houses, trees, cattle, people. It would destroy lives, hit vehemently on the banks, cracking and shattering the soil beneath, and then pulling the land toward her, leaving its inhabitants homeless, landless. The river always destroyed existing lands in passionate intensity, just the way it created new ones, ripping lands from one side and storing them inside while germinating fertile soil on which would rise a new civilization. The new island that he saw forming by the riverside would not make a permanent or inhabitable land, he knew. He could read it in the very formation of the new land, the texture of its soil and the aquatic plants that grew in it, and in the tidal waves. That land would submerge in the water very soon. He would not waste time by putting a claim on the newly risen islet.

His life ran parallel to these islands that he had under his possession. The river of his life never had a set course and yet never ceased creating new landforms out of a mere nothingness. His life followed the course of its own tidal waves; like the river, it ran upward, got stagnant a few times, and then retrieved its force. He had to look back twice to take one step ahead. Life is a monkey trying to climb an oily bamboo pole and slipping through it; ascending two feet, slipping down one foot and then ascending two feet again. A relentless climber, Life is. But which one is life? The slippery bamboo pole, or the relentless monkey? Helaluddin's face saw a smirk of self-satisfaction, reflecting on this intelligent analogy.

What he experienced as life was never an easy one: he had to witness and cause bloodshed in his search and claims for new islands; he had been through everything—death, arrests, sufferings of families, police harassments. He had to oversee everything, and at every step, he feared for his own life, dreading a dismal end of life or honor, property, and people. But it did not begin that way. He had spent a happy childhood. His father owned a retail business of spices. He used to spend his days with his father at the retail store by the train station at Jamtayl, a place that was about three miles away from the village where they lived. He always enjoyed those days that he spent with his father. Going to the store itself was a joyous event. They had to travel on horseback. Once they reached the store, employees always threw a tantrum to please the owner's son. Siraj Mian, the manager of the store would send someone to the Dessert store at the nearby bazaar to get the best kinds of Gulab jamun, gilebi, and chamcham. They pampered him with food and dessert, praise and attention, and he enjoyed every moment of it. Shipments of cardamoms, cinnamons, bay leaves, raisins, nuts, cloves, nutmegs, and maces came from all over the places. His father's store was the sole distributor of *garam masala* in that area and the store stayed busy during the Eid and Pooja festivities. The young Helaluddin would take his seat on a fluffy cushion and eat a handful of raisins, watching the commotion of people at his father's store and the hustling trains at the nearby rail station. He had no watch on him, but he could easily tell time hearing the whistles of the trains; he knew exactly at what time of the day each cargo train reached the station. The moment he heard the stationmaster ring the bell to announce the arrival of a passenger train, he would feel restless and run to the station to watch the hustle and bustle of the station and the looming dust that outran an approaching train and reached the station first. The big train uncoiled and moved like a big snake, as it came to Jamtayl, from Iswardi Junction. He had been on this train with his father and his younger sister Helena. Traveling with Father was always a luxurious event: he could enjoy the comfort of first-class compartments, eat everything he wanted from the wandering vendors at every station—hot tea, boiled egg, chanachur, and puffed rice, lozenges. In every station where the train halted, the passengers rushed in, and so did the vendors, carrying their delicacies on a tray or in boxes or hotspots. Ah! Those hard-boiled eggs, peeled by some unwashed hands, and then delivered in a torn piece of old newspaper, sprinkled with a little salt and red pepper, and some roadside dirt, of course. Helaluddin could still relish that taste—inside his mouth, his memory.

Ugh, the bitter taste of Neem twig! Helaluddin came back to his present moment—sitting by the bank of the river and brushing his teeth with a Neem twig toothbrush. He spat on the dirt and stood up. He had been sitting for a long time. He watched the morning fog gradually lifting its blanket as he started walking by the bank, at a slow pace. Two human shapes slowly emerged from the disappearing blanket of fog and walked towards him, being totally unaware of his presence at that hour of the morning.

"Who's that?" Helaluddin shouted. "Hey, who's there? Who are you?"

The two men startled and turned back and started walking away from him.

"Who are you? Hey, why don't you speak? Speak! Stop, STOP! Hey!"

The two started running, and Helaluddin ran in a futile attempt to catch them. Who were those people? What were they doing on his island at such an hour? Were they spying? Were they trying to create havoc? Were they Mojnu's spies? Did they come here on behalf of a new claimant of his land? Helaluddin's forehead wrinkled with all these questions. He had to find out the truth behind all these, he told himself, as he rushed back home.

"Let's go to the city, to Rajapur," Helaluddin proposed to Surat Ali after he finished his breakfast. He took a large portmanteau with him. Surat Ali knew they did not need extra sets of clothes or a large amount of money for a short trip to the city, but it was not his nature to ask unnecessary questions. He just followed his boss and walked behind him on their way to Rajapur.

They reached the city by noon and stopped by Shuja Mian's Tea stall to grab a quick cup of tea.

"Take a seat, Mr. Talukdar, I am going to make you the best tea, with cream that I prepared myself from the purest milk."

"Yeah, right. I am sure you mixed a jug of water to give that milk its purest form," someone teased.

"Hey, back off, man! Don't insult me like that! I will never treat Mr. Talukdar with disrespect as you are suggesting!"

"Calm down," Helaluddin said. "Water evaporates when you boil the milk for a long time. So it doesn't matter if you mixed water with milk."

"Take a listen to the words of a wise man, you goons!" Shuja Mian approached his honored guest with his best cup of tea.

"Shuja Mian, have you lately seen Mojnu from Betel? Does he come to your stall?"

"Ha, Mr. Talukdar, he was here just the other day. Came with Mr. Matin. Do you know Mojnu has suddenly changed his attitude? He's trying to be so important a man just because he hangs out with people like Mr. Matin."

Helaluddin chatted with Shuja Mian and other customers at his tea stall for a long time, asking them random questions, laughing at irrelevant jokes, in an effort to find some clues about the morning strangers on his island.

"We will go to the main town now, Surat Ali," he finally decided.

"Want to catch the train, or should I rent a bicycle from Mustafa's store?"

"We won't be able to make it to the station on time, and I don't feel like cycling now. Rent a big boat instead."

They reached the town by boat. It was almost the end of the day when they reached their destination: the office cum residence of Mr. Sanwar, the lawyer. The Lawyer had turned the front room of his house into his office. His legal assistant, Harmuz Ali, managed the office for him. Helaluddin always stayed on good terms with Harmuz Ali because he knew at times, the legal Assistant could be more useful than the lawyer. Harmuz Ali was quite happy to see Helaluddin and went inside to inform the lawyer of his arrival.

The lawyer gave Helaluddin and his companion a warm welcome.

"What brought you to the town?" He asked.

"My dear lawyer, I thought I should inform you that Mojnu, from the village Betil, is planning to take possession of my island. And he is being backed by Matin."

"Which Matin?"

"The one affiliated with the Muslim League. I think we should do something about it."

Sanwar, the Lawyer coughed. He looked both worried and excited.

"Why are you always worried about your isles? Think beyond your islands, your properties. There are more things in this world than your islands, and these people are after them too! They won't stop only by snatching your lands. They will go after more important things. They are getting organized to commit more crimes, but you know what? We are getting organized as well! We are making our own plans—to speak of our rights, to claim our rights. We are aware of the growing disparities between West Pakistan and us. And we need to make the common people aware of all these inequalities. Very soon, there will be a parliamentary election, and I know the conniving Matin will orchestrate a bigger offense."

"But what should we do?"

"Talk to the people of your precinct, your village. Make them aware of their political rights. I know most of the villagers do not exercise their right to vote; I'm not even sure if they know that they have that right. Inform them—of their power, their rights—tell the way they are being discriminated against. Arrange a few public speaking events and invite me to give speeches. I will talk to people. I will tell them what they should know. I will also send my political workers to work at the grass-root level. These are politically active student leaders that I will send to your village to speak to your people. They will tell the villagers what to do, how to organize a political event; they will train the villagers to run such events. And don't worry about the expenses, it wouldn't be your headache, it'll be taken care of; you just organize the event. People should know how they are being deprived of their rights, how the West Pakistani Government is oppressing them, making them suffer—politically, financially, culturally—they are hurting us in all possible levels that they can! If you arrange such public speaking events, then you will be doubly benefitted: you will be able to take the lead in making people aware of the oppression imposed by West Pakistan, and you will be able to send a message to Mojnu and Matin's team—that you have our support. That will be quite a shock for them."

Helaluddin was aware of the changing waves of time, and he knew Tota and his fighter group would not be able to give him protection anymore. Time was spreading its wings with shifting colors everywhere. Once, he only needed Tota Mian to bring his team of pole fighters to claim and maintain his possessions over the islands. But now, conniving people like Mojnus and Matins roamed freely everywhere, threatening to topple the balance of power. And now, he would have the wise guidance of Mr. Sanwar, the Lawyer, to help him tackle all troubles. Now was the time to bathe in the stream of excitement of a new kind— an elation that might bring something bigger than some land newly risen from the belly of a fertile river.

"Freeing yourself was one thing, claiming ownership of that freed self was another."

— <u>Toni Morrison</u>

Chapter 8
The Never-ending Game of Pole

In remote villages, sports and entertainment were rare occurrences in winter. The one game that could pull Noor Mohammad out of the comfort of a warm blanket in a winter day was the thrill of watching a pole-fighting tournament. Noor Mohammad woke up to that excitement one morning as the rhythmic drum beats of a pole fighter team rumbled through the village. First, the beat came slow and soft, but then gradually it became louder and kept getting stronger, thudding and hammering, and pounding, until it pulled the whole village out in the open sky, in search of its source. Children would start running, and screaming women would chase after their children, men—old and young—all would come out, askance:

Where is it beating from? Which house is having this pole-fighting event?
Hey, boy, ask someone, what's the venue.
Who should I ask?
Ask someone. Call someone.

Who will hear me amidst this conundrum? Get your dick out of your ear and pay attention. Can't you hear the loud drumbeat?

Hey, shut up boy, behave! Why are you cursing? What the fuck?

The overpowering sound of drumbeats would diminish the bickering crowd by the time Noor Mohammad would join them. He would run and scream with the moving crowd in search of the source. No one would stop him or call him back; no one, except the Moulavi, from the *Madrassa*. He would chastise him for acting up like an ignorant child:

"Don't you know this pole fighting game is a Hindu tradition? How can you—being a Quran Hafiz—debase yourself by attending such a Hindu sport?"

Sometimes Noor Mohammad considered this—this being a Hafiz in the Quran – his ultimate crime! Just because he knew the whole Quran by heart did not mean that he had no right to enjoy the small pleasures of life that boys of his age so easily enjoyed. He felt guilty for his divine knowledge, as he felt guilty for being the nephew of a powerful man. But this powerful man of the village never scorned him or scolded him if he did not go to the *Madrassa* regularly or if he was not punctual about his daily prayers. Uncle Helal wouldn't chastise him if he followed the crowd to the source of the drum rhythm. Noor Mohammad gleefully ran with the rest of the crowd and reached the house of Uncle Harmuz, where the tournament started a few weeks ago. And this morning, he ran to his own house, the house where the players were setting up for the concluding session of the whole event. It was customary to end the performance in the courtyard of the powerful Mr. Helaluddin Talukdar.

By the time Noor Mohammad reached his house, people had already formed a circle around the two pole-fighters, Sujan and Hobibar, who were standing at the center of the circle, ready to start the event. Band of drummers stood inside the circle, rhythmically beating wooden and clay drums that they hung on their shoulder, with a long piece of cloth. Sujan and Hobibar would start prancing with the drumbeat, each holding and moving along and thin bamboo pole, whipping it in the air like a sword. They would prance and swing the thin pole at each other, trying to hit and hurt the opponent, trying to dodge a lash. They would jump and hop, sway and swing, from left to right, right to left, aiming at the opponent with a thin bamboo rod. Their pace would be controlled by the drumbeat: slow when the beat was slow and soft, and aggressive and attacking when the beat sped up. The crowd would clap and scream to provoke and inspire the fighters. At one point, with the appearance of the lead entertainer, the two would drop their bamboo rods and invite each other to a friendly embrace. Tota Mian was always the lead performer. His bamboo pole was markedly different from the rest. Each sheath scar on the sturdy stem was adorned with a brass ring that sparkled in the sun; each internode was polished and smoothed with oil, giving the whole cylindrical stem an invincible look. Total Mian stood at the center and displayed his mastery. He threw his pole in the air and grabbed it before it touched the earth. He aimed at the sun with his spear and pulled it back at him; he juggled the long stem with such velocity, that for a moment the crowd felt hypnotized, as if hallucinating an agile body with six hands, juggling a spear with utmost speed and ferocity, like the Goddess Durga.

The performers then went from house to house, showing their skills with the weapon, and the crowd followed. The homeowners offered puffed rice and molasses to the drummers and the pole-fighters. At night, the game would change its course and get a bit violent, with some players performing with a burning bamboo stem and some inflicting wounds on their body by hitting their bare chests with long metal blades. They would pause occasionally to take a sip of water or a bite of food. The only weapons that would beat nonstop were the hands of the drummers. They would not disrupt the rhythm or give their drums any rest. They would only pause if requested by the host or interrupted by any spontaneous singer who wanted to share his emotions about the festivities, about this winter sport of pole fighting that kept the whole village awake and in spirit.

I played my bamboo pole
With the rhythm of the dhol
You cast your glance at me one day, the way peeps
Green ash gourd through its hanging leaves
I saw your face, but I did not see
You, when you fixed your eyes on me.
O, my whole life is all done,
And yet, the game of pole that I play is an unending one.

The song would invoke some sort of spiritual feeling among some audience, while some others, driven by their jealousy of a rendition offered by such a young singer, would divert people's attention to the main event—the pole-fight. "Aren't we here to enjoy the skillful display of bamboo-pole handling? Let's see more of that and stop singing!" They would say.

The last event of this pole-fight festivity always took place in their courtyard. The whole courtyard lit by kerosene Tiki torches. The main attraction was always the concluding *Hazra* performance by Altab Mandal. He smeared his body with dark coal and limestone and woe a wig made of shiny jute fiber. He held a long machete and sat at the center of the crowd, occasionally spinning the machete over his head while making an uncanny ear-piercing sound. A group of pole fighters formed a small circle around a man who was buried alive, vertically up to his neck on the ground. This man's life depended on the Hazra performance of Altab Mandal. Altab would have to bring a fresh skull and release the buried man from the spell of an evil spirit. The man would be left there to die if Altab failed to bring a skull within a certain time.

The semi-buried man was exhausted with fear and anxiety. The drummers relentlessly beat their dhols, and the hyped-up crowd clapped their hands and screamed their hearts. Amidst all these, Altab Mian jumped and spun his machete over his head and twirled it at the crowd and screamed like an animal. Then all of a sudden, he would run, sprint through the crowd and vanish in the dark. The pole-fighters stood in a semi-circle around the half-buried man and clicked and clanked their bamboo shaft in a rhythmic pattern. The crowd sat aghast, anticipating the worse fate for the half-buried man, expecting Altab Mandal to complete his role as a savior. But Altab Mandal did not show up. People spent hours weaving stories of his bravery.

And Altab Mandal remained absent from the scene. The night was ready to depart and the half-buried man was ready to give up. It was only then the crowd screamed happiness! "He is coming! He is bringing the *Hazra*! Don't you hear him coming?"

Altab Mandal came back with a skull, freshly procured from somewhere—maybe the Kali Temple, or maybe from the Hindu crematory. This was not an easy task; he had to battle the djinns and evil spirits, and he had to fight with the Goddess Kali just to obtain a skull fresh enough to save a fresh life. As Altab Mandal entered the circle holding a human skull with one hand and his machete with the other, the bamboo pole-fighter group dug the almost unconscious body out of his grave and pushed him toward Altab Mandal. The man, as if in a trance, ran to Altab, grabbed the skull from his hand, and incessantly rubbed his forehead on the skull. The dhol started beating to its utmost rhythm and its highest sound until it suddenly stopped. Altab Mandal had saved the man and thus saved the spirit of the pole-fighting event for that year. He would have to do it again next winter.

The circle dismantled, and the crowd walked toward the first rays of dawn. Noor Mohammad also stood up to go back inside. He had been enjoying this sport every winter, and he clearly remembered believing Altab Mandal and his performance to be real. He always felt empathy for the man whose life depended on the success of Altab Mandal and like everyone else, he also used to admire Altab for his heroism. But this year, to his amazement, he found the whole incident to be too artificial; he could see through the performances of the man buried in the hole in their courtyard, the pole-fighters prancing around him, and the fierce-looking *Hazra* seeker. The only true sensation was created by the bamboo-pole fight and the rhythmic drumbeats. Everything else seemed unimpressive to him and did not attract him anymore. He was changing, he suddenly realized. He was changing, and so was his concept of faith and disbelief.

"You can't find someone who doesn't want to be found."
– <u>Isabel Allende</u>

Chapter 9

Strangers in the Island

Strangers always came to his island, in search of a house to live in, a piece of land to till on, to give life a chance to survive. Sometimes they worked for food or borrowed money and sometimes they leased the farming land, but most of the time they, failed to pay back in the beginning. The island soil was quite fertile: certain parts of the island were perfect for cultivating paddy, and most of the land was good for growing all sorts of lentils and legumes—Urad, Toor, Chickpeas, couscous, and corn. Helaluddin kept the most fertile part of the land for growing paddy and let the rest to be used by the new settlers. Growing crops on the island was never easy; floods, land erosions, monsoon rains, and seasonal storms—anything or all could disrupt and destroy the crops. Living an easy and respectable life was also not a given factor. Nature was not the only adversary for the new settlers here. People from the mainland always looked down upon them, called them drifters, slighted their hands in marriage, and questioned their knowledge in every aspect. Helaluddin tried to amend those by establishing schools, madrassas, and mosques. He was always tireless in his attempt to help people build a piece of their own world in this land that floated on the river's belly. A little world of their own—his own—that was all he aspired to. But why would he need a world of his own? Why would anyone want that? What good would that bring? What would be the purpose—of one's own world, or one's life? Why were all these hankerings after the world and all that belonged in it? Why was the rush and why couldn't this rush just cease to be? Why would people like him or Naimuddi still need to run and seek for new lands and new homes? Naimuddi, a potential new settler, had come from a faraway village and brought with him his daughter Zayeda and the three-year-old granddaughter.

Naimuddi's wife had passed away when their daughter was ten-years-old, and he had been taking care of his daughter since then. When Zayeda grew up into a strong and beautiful woman, Naimuddi sold his house and all belongings just so he was able to pay the dowry for her marriage. But that marriage did not last long.

They used to beat her, always, and whenever. At one point in her abusive married life, Zayeda just kicked her husband in between his two legs. Naimuddi told him how Zayeda's husband threw a tantrum after being kicked in his balls. The bastard provoked his male family members to thrash Zayeda for her misdeed. He kicked her out of the house as punishment. Zayeda came back to her father's house and brought along a newborn baby girl. But Naimuddi was totally broke by then and had no other options but to seek a job and a home in Helaluddin's new island. Helaluddin gave Naimuddi a piece of land and asked him to build his own home there. He hired Zayeda to work as a maid in his house and help Helena in her works.

Helaluddin never got married. He was leaving a life of a perfect bachelor. People had been uselessly trying to work as his matchmaker; they brought him news of marriageable girls, showed her pictures, or directly called out at him, "who would keep your name alive once you are dead?" But Helaluddin absorbed every query nonchalantly and commented that his life was not a smooth one, and he would not make a woman's life miserable just in the name of marriage. But was it really the truth? Helaluddin wondered! Wouldn't marriage be a good solution—to all problems and help him suppress all unmentionable and unfixable fractions of the real truth? Naimuddi's new dreams of a new home instilled this sudden pondering in Helaluddin—about a new life as a married man. Helaluddin spread the reed mattress under the shade of the big Jackfruit tree and lay down on his back. Up above him, the sky laid bare its star-studded canopy for his visual pleasure. He looked up and followed the dazzling paths and designs created by those stars.

He still remembered the day Helena taught him how to watch the stars. It was during the "Gassi" festival in one autumn. As it was the custom, the unmarried girls of the village ground fresh rice flour and soaked it in water, made rice cake balls and arranged them in wicker baskets; they then put their baskets on rooftop overnight under open sky, to be dipped by the dews and chill winds of autumn, for the special added taste. The girls would then wander in groups: scavenging for the tallest Shonda stems. One with the tallest stem was sure to have the longest hair in the future. After collecting the long Shonda stems, the girls made a herbal paste of masoor lentil and dub it over their hair and sat all night, holding the Shonda stems in their hand and guarding the growth of hair on their heads and the wicker basket full of rice cake balls that were soaking in night dews on rooftops.

Boys of the village in the meantime had their own festivities to run, and that did not involve making or growing anything. They would group up and try to steal the wicker baskets. Those rice cake balls were after all a delicious treat. If the girls caught them in the process of stealing, they would have to accept the punishment, a cruel punishment of course: they had to sit all night by the river bank and guard the girls as they dived into the river holding the Shonda stem with their two hands, and then bathed for a long time in the river just to wash off the herbal paste from their hair.

That autumn, Helena was in charge of guarding the wicker baskets. The boys selected Helaluddin to be their messenger and asked him to spy on the girls and gather information. As Helaluddin walked into the yard, he saw his younger sister Helena and her friend Mariam lying on the ground, with their eyes fixed—not at the rooftop baskets, but at the starry sky.

"Hi! Helena, what are you guys doing?" Helaluddin remembered asking his younger sister.

"Nothing; guarding the rice cake balls. Come watch the sky with us, see how beautiful it is," she said.

Helaluddin sat down on the mattress.

"Lie down, or you won't be able to see clearly."

Helaluddin lay down beside his sister and watched what they were watching, with utter amazement. The whole sky was like a big canopy, lit with golden stars. The stars were spread all over the canopy like a masterpiece crafted by some expert artists. He kept his gaze fixed on the starry canopy as he lay between Helena and Mariam. Time stood still as he watched the stars. His eyes, his mind, his whole being stayed motionless in the act of stargazing. His leg accidentally touched Mariam's and felt a surging spark that ran through his veins. Mariam did not move. She let her foot stay still as his leg touched hers and caressed without moving any limbs. He could spend the whole night just like that if only Helena did not startle him: "Look, there's someone trying to steal our cakes!" Helaluddin jumped up on his feet and ran with the boys. Years had passed since then, but he still remembered that night, the spark that ran through his blood when his feet touched Mariam's feet. Every time he saw Mariam after that night, all he could think of was her feet and felt his blood running through his vein in an attempt to explode inside. A few years later, during another Gassi night, Mariam took her pair of thrilling feet to the river to perform the bathing festival and did not come out. Helena was the first one to notice that Mariam was missing. One minute she was with them in the river and the next minute she was gone. Villagers formed a search team and dived into the water; they threw fishing nets everywhere and finally caught her body in one of the nets, wrapped in riverweeds and grass. Aquatic grassroots spread their roots like ropes and tied down her two feet together. Helaluddin went to see Mariam—lying dead, covered with a white sheet, only her two feet were showing. Those two feet…dead and yet still produced the same thrilling sensation in him.

Someone touched his feet.

"Who is here?"

"It's only me, Zayeda. Just putting a shawl over your legs. Looked like you were feeling cold."

"Oh, okay." Helaluddin sat down. He forgot how long he'd been lying there under the open sky.

"Need anything?"

"No."

"You want to go inside and lie down? I will rub oil on your feet, or I can give you a massage. Do you want that?"

"No, Zayeda, I don't need any of those. Go to your room."

Zyeda sat down quietly. She stayed there with him for a few moments. None of them said a word. He did not move as she let out a sigh and left.

Helaluddin lay down again, looking at the starry sky. What are these stars, really? How many stars are there? Are they really the souls of dead folks, blinking their way till eternity? Do souls really live after the body's demise? Do they turn into stars, or do they go somewhere else and wait to be resurrected on the Day of Judgment? Do the souls come back in the form of a new life? Do they come back to complete the purgatorial journey? Does anything remain after death to experience the purgatory of hell and the heavenly bliss? Do people come back and relive eternal pain or pleasure? How? Dust goes to dust, then what or how a concrete shape comes back from that dust? The stars of the canopy-sky lighted these thoughts inside his head, with their blinking sparks and Helaluddin let them grow. The stars. If people want to become stars, then which of these was Mariam? How would he recognize her? A meteor rose and fell somewhere as if it was the answer to his question.

"We all owe death a life."

— <u>Salman Rushdie</u>

Chapter 10

Bereaving Time

Such torrential rain! If it could, the sky would grow a tender sore from such ceaseless outpour! Helaluddin sat by the window and watched the cascade of rainfall as he listened to its rhythmic beat, munching on the freshly puffed rice that Zayeda had prepared for him with a hint of salt, a dash of mustard oil, and some thinly chopped green chili pepper. He could hear Helena's intermittent groan and started feeling restless. The sound of the rhythmic rain was not strong enough to suppress the feeling of unrest that the growl inflicted on him. Time, a quisling mole, tapping and unmasking what he thought he had forgotten a long while ago. But nothing seemed to have faded with time. Memories of his childhood. The bygone days of unforgettable sorrows and immeasurable happiness.

That autumn, their river was swollen with fish. He was fourteen then, and Helena, a few years younger. He and Helena had a sister in between them, but the poor girl did not survive long enough to be a part of the bond. Helaluddin was the only son of his parents—the family beacon, as they called him. So that autumn, the fourteen-year-old Helaluddin saw the surge of fish—a river with its belly full of fish of all kinds! They could catch fish even by spreading a cheesecloth in place of a fishing net. It went to a point where the whole village felt overtaken and exhausted; they could not eat fish anymore. So the next step was drying them by making fish wreaths and drying them in the open sun and preserve it for future use. The village smelled of fried fish, cooked fish, dried fish, fishbone, fish scales, and rotten fish.

"God knows what these village people will bring on to them through this massive fish consumption!" Helaluddin's father used to complain. Helaluddin was too ignorant to understand the implication of that statement until he saw it with his own eyes. Within a few days, Hashem Sheikh's son was taken by *Olabibi* one night and died before dawn.

"And here it comes," his father sadly said, "*Olabibi,* the bearer of the cholera epidemic."

Helaluddin's father ordered his servants to collect the wreaths of dried fish, raw fish, and fish waste from every house and dump those in a deep hole and then cover the hole with dirt and gravel. But that did not put an end to *Olabibi*'s adventure. Hashem Shekh's wife and granddaughter were attacked next and were quickly taken away by Olabibi—the woman in white that walked like a night's shadow from one house to another. Any house that fell under her shadow must respond to her call: vomit, diarrhea, death—these became an endless chain of reaction to the call. Yelling, lamenting, and screaming was all one could hear from a house that received a visit from the woman in a white sari.

The epidemic gradually spread all over the village, and not a single house remained unaffected. Helaluddin's mother proposed to leave the village, but his father opposed it. They would be okay if she followed proper health and hygiene rules, he told her. But he was wrong. The village became a haunted grave soon; no one came out, and no one cried or yelled for help. The living ones, stayed inside trying their best to keep their grip over life as tightly as they could while the dead ones were left in the open. The cemeteries ran out of burial ground, and the people ran out of courage to mourn and bury their dead, and then started the hysterical exodus. People started to flee, toward cities, toward hope.

"I wish I had taken your suggestion," his father told his mother, "we should have left the village; in fact, let us leave for the city tomorrow." But as Olabibi visited their house and took one of their maids the next morning, the rest of the crew fled. Inside the house, their mother held their father closer as he took in the attack, like a hero.

"Take the kids to the city, and don't worry about me," he kept telling his wife, but she did not leave him. She ordered Helaluddin to take his sister away and sit tight in another room. No matter what happened, he should not come out and check. From their room, the two siblings could hear their parents taking care of each other as both fell victim to cholera. All night long, they heard their parents regretting and lamenting for not leaving the village when there was still time. Soon, their voices grew weak, and the children could not hear anymore, for they fell asleep, hoping to find their parents alive and healthy under the morning sun. But the morning came with bucketing rain, and the siblings went to the adjacent room to find their mother sleeping peacefully, resting her head over their father's chest, with no intention of waking up ever.

The rain prevented them from going out, and there was no one to ask help from. Helaluddin and his sister sat by the corner of the bed as their parents slept their eternal sleep. The two lay down by the feet of their parents and waited. Days went by one after another and took their nights with them, but the siblings did not move. They lay there like corpses and let time pass. They had no hunger, no thirst, and no desire to wake up. Their lips got chapped and dry, their dried lips bled, and they had no strength to stir a limb. On the third day, Helaluddin woke up and saw his sister lying unconscious beside him, hugging him as tight as possible, and he saw his parents lying stiff in another corner of the same bed. First, he was not sure whether she was dead or alive. He sat up and saw the decomposing bodies of his parents. He looked outside and saw a bright day for the rain had stopped. He gabbed Helena by her hand and stepped outside. Then they ran through the deserted road, toward an unknown destination before being stopped by a group of masked men riding a bullock carriage.

"Where are you coming from, kids? Is anyone else alive in your house?"

Helaluddin made a hand gesture to point in the direction of their house and fell unconscious on the ground.

He woke up in a hospital bed a few days later but did not see Helena by his side.

"Where am I? Where is my little sister?" He asked the nurse.

"You are safe, don't worry. You are in hospital. Your sister is safe too. She is resting in another bed."

"The rescue team arranged for the burial of your parents." She told him. "But do you have any living relative? Do you know where they live?"

Helaluddin cried his heart out: Who would take care of them? Who were the living relatives that would take them in? Who were those people? Their mother was the only child, and their maternal grandparents died long ago. He did not know of any relative from his father's side except for some distant ones. But those distant relatives would only come to ask for monetary favors from the father and were of no good. Helaluddin realized he and Helena had no one to lean on.

"You have been discharged and ready to go home," the Nurse told Helaluddin a few days later.

"Going home, where?" He was confused.

"With your uncle, he's been waiting for you two." Helaluddin held his sister's hand and came out. He saw a man signing the release forms on their behalf. The man looked at them and smiled. Helaluddin cringed inside as the smile instantly brought back some unpleasant memories. He vaguely remembered seeing this man a long time ago, one winter, raising a feud with his father over something.

"Let's go, children," said the stranger. "Our boat is ready to set sail!" As the three of them reached the riverbank, Helaluddin saw the big boat awaiting their arrival. When he was young, he used to love Kader Ali's harrowing tales of piracy and robbery. One such story was about a band of merchants carrying their shipment by the boat. At the death of a chilly night, the crew of that big commercial boat decided to get rid of the merchant. Gagged him, and tied him with ropes, and pushed him in the river.

The band of boatmen then rowed away with a boat full of merchandise. Every time Helaluddin heard that story, he had an uncanny empathy for the drowned merchant. He experienced the same uncanny fear once again as the new Uncle led them to his boat.

The big boat was nicely decorated inside, with soft cushion beds and pillows to rest on, water pitcher and food baskets neatly arranged, just to give its passengers a homely feeling. As Helaluddin and Helena got on board, the Uncle asked someone to bring a basket full of puffed rice and dried sugar balls for them.

"Eat and relax," he told them. "You may have not recognized me, but I am your closest relative, the only brother—step though—that your father had. Eat and stay comfortable; we will have to travel with this boat for about two days to reach my village, your new home."

For two days and two nights, Helaluddin and Helena lived on the boat, ate chicken curry, rice and vegetable dishes that were cooked by the boatmen, and slept in one corner of the boat, always anticipating danger, always afraid. But nothing bad happened. The journey was in fact pleasant. After every few hours, the boatmen would anchor the big boat and go to the village bazaar to gather live chicken, fish, or vegetables. They then prepared the food and fed them properly: Helaluddin could still remember the taste of delicious chicken curry that the boatmen cooked! After they reached the riverbank, their Uncle got into a bullock driven cart with them, and they traveled for half a day in that cart. The final destination was a nice house in a new village—the Uncle's house—a house full of curious people. Everyone wanted to know about them, and everyone wanted to talk. The Uncle introduced them to his family members, and asked them to welcome two new family members. Helaluddin felt safe, being surrounded by his late father's family. Helena sat stiffly by Helaluddin, motionless, reactionless, and speechless.

The Village was called Shimultali, Helaluddin came to know later, but he could not recognize its location. Was it in the same district as their own village? Was it on the north or south side of the town? How far did they travel? How far were they from their own homes? Helaluddin made a futile effort for the first few days to figure out the location and direction of Shimultali to and from his own home and then he gave up There was no use trying. The house was full of compassionate people, the new Aunt tried her best to make Helena comfortable in the house, and Helaluddin had no worries about food or shelter. He managed to feel at home, but troubles started with Helena. She became clingy. She would not let Helaluddin go out of sight; she would not eat with others or would not sleep at night in another room. Most of the nights she, would scream and yell and woke up the whole household. The nocturnal screams were just the beginning. Next came her hallucinations. She started seeing things around her, attacking her, and over her.

"Help! A snake is slithering all over me!" She cried one night. The whole house woke up and started looking for the snake that was nowhere to be found. The night hallucination was followed by other signs. She started talking to herself, whispering, and chuckling, chatting—gibberish. She did not trust anyone, never befriended anyone, and never wanted to be approached by any compassionate heart. The new Aunt knew what was ailing this little girl; she was still at a loss and still trying to cope up with the new life, she said. As a temporary solution, she offered to let Helena stay close to her in a room adjacent to hers so that she could supervise. Helaluddin was asked to share a bedroom with his male cousins on the outskirt of the yard across from the main house.

One night, Helaluddin woke up to find Helena lying by him in his bed, trembling and sobbing.

"Save me, brother!"

"What, what happened?" Helaluddin muttered in sleep.

"Save me, please, save me!"

"What, tell me? Tell me what happened. Save you from what?"

"Brother, save me. Take me away from here. Save me from the new uncle."

Helaluddin woke up, alert and ready, like a hunter. He grabbed his sister's hand, and together they ran as fast as they could, as far away as possible, from that ominous darkness, in the direction of a safety unbeknownst.

"I am a cage, in search of a bird."

— <u>Franz Kafka</u>

Chapter 11
Life Ablaze

Noor Mohammad was trying to finish his homework assignments for Pundit Khagen. Bengali, World History, Math, and Geography. With his academic skills, he could easily have gotten into the Boarding School in town. But his mother! She was the one who did not want him to go away even though Uncle Helaluddin was eager to send him there for his education. Now he was stuck in the village, under the supervision of one Moulavi, who taught him religious studies and one Pundit who taught him liberal arts, math, and science, and had to get his head stuck in the whirlwind of contradiction! The knowledge that the Moulavi provided for him stood in eternal conflict with the ones derived from the Pundit's erudition. Answers didn't match; information clashed, and he grew more confused than enlightened. His photographic memory only helped him remember every bit of information without providing him with answers to resolve all conflicts that arose from the learning. Asya, the maid stepped in and told him Mother's rice pancakes were ready.

Noor Mohammad jumped off and ran to the kitchen. Mother's rice pancakes! Made from freshly ground rice that was soaked in water and then cooked in the shape of round cakes. Then those pancakes were soaked overnight in milk, boiled with the sweet sap collected from the date trees. The pancakes soaked in milk and sweet syrup all night long and were ready to be devoured in the morning. Sometimes Mother did not soak them in milk; she sometimes served some of those cakes warm and fresh from frying pan, with soft molasses. Uncle Helal loved that treat. Noor Mohammad sat by his mother as she kept herself busy flipping, the pancakes and storing them in a clay pot.

"Homework is done, kiddo?" The mother asked.

"Yes." Noor Mohammad sat beside his mother.

"Want some molasses?"

"No." He took a rice pancake and broke it in half.

"Are you sad?"

"No."

"You look lost, I can see. You can't deceive a mother's eye."

"But mother, you can't answer the questions that are killing me."

"True."

"Why didn't you go to school, Mother?"

"I don't know," she sighed. "Guess I didn't like school; I'd rather play with my friends all day long instead of going to school."

"Hmm."

"But, my dear child, not having an education has given me the power to contain my questions. I don't ask useless questions that no one knows how to answer."

Noor Mohammad looked at his mother's face, glowing and reflecting the radiance of the burning flames from the clay stove. How beautiful she looked!

"Mother, I am going out to take a stroll by the river."

Life always brings a new shade, add a new meaning to it. Same things look new, and same experience seems unique every time it happens. Trees that he looked at every day while taking a stroll by the river looked the same and yet anew. Those trees, the haystack, those birds chirping on the branches of those same old trees, those little half-naked children playing in the dirt looked elegantly unique every time he looked at them. Every single time.

Noor Mohammad sat by the river and looked yonder. The villages on the other side of the river stood like a smudged shadow. Up above, the clouds changed their shapes with every stroke of gentle air. Clouds became creatures of different kinds—horses, elephants, and sometimes humans. Noor Mohammad enjoyed watching the shape-shifting clouds constantly changing, constantly reforming into the shapes of animals, humans, objects. They then turned into something else. The clouds suddenly started to spread through the sky, in flaming shapes of fire: one, two, three, four, five, six, and seven. The setting sun left its tinge on each of those seven flame-shaped clouds as if ignited with fire. The fiery cloud slowly spread its flames all over the sky in an attempt to set the whole sky ablaze. Was the sky going to burn in its own cloud-fire? Khagen Pundit taught him about the fire and about how to locate its origin. You could read the purpose of fire from its location, he had told him. A fire set toward the east would mean it was a sacrificial offering to the gods; a South facing fire would be lit in honor of the departed souls, and the west-facing fire flames would come from cooking purpose. The seven fiery flames of clouds spread their wings in the sky, over his head, like a blazing canopy. The whole sky was on fire and the flames were coming after him. Noor Mohammad dived into the river to dodge the blazing flame.

"I am rooted, but I flow."

– <u>*Virginia Woolf*</u>

Chapter 12

Who is Close to your Heart, and Who is Afar?

Helaluddin was running, and Helena was running with him. They held each other's hand and kept running, away, as far away possible, from Shimultali. They had been running since midnight and hadn't had the courage to stop. The night ended and the sun peeped through morning sky, but they still did not quit running. The morning sun went brighter and brighter, and they still kept running. The scorching sun reached the mid sky, and Helena ran out of breath. "I am thirsty, brother. Need a drink of water," she said. Helaluddin could hear a train whistling just a few yards away and implored his sister to hold up a little longer. "We will wait at the train station," he said and asked her to run in the direction of the sound. The sun almost was ready to quit the day by the time they reached the station. They drank water from a public tube well.

"Brother, I am hungry."

"Then let's go eat something from any street-side hotel."

The name of the train station was Haripur. Helaluddin had heard of this rail station from their father so many times. Their father used to bring his merchandize from Darjeeling on a cargo train via this station. He had heard about this station so many times that he felt as if he had been here before, walked around the platform, or hopped on one of those trains already. He took Helena to a nearby restaurant and ordered rice and mutton curry. Since they were quite well dressed, Helena and him had no problem waiting for those children from a well off family. Helaluddin and Helena ate to their heart's content. Helena was shocked when Helaluddin paid the bill.

"Where did you get the money?" She asked the moment they were out of the restaurant.

"Took it from Cousin Nazmul's wallet."

"You stole money? You?"

"Well, let's call it a loan. I borrowed without his knowledge and will return the money when I get my own." He said with confidence as he walked toward the station.

"Why are we going to the station, brother?"

"Because we are getting on a train."

"Aren't you going to buy the tickets?"

"No."

Helaluddin helped Helena get in the train compartment and started searching for an empty seat. From the looks of him, no one would have guessed that he had embarked the train without having any specific destination in mind.

Helaluddin had heard the names of train stations around this area. He decided to get off at the farthest one. It was night already, and there seemed to be no ticket checker present on that train; Helaluddin and his sister had an uninterrupted journey. They slept through the night and woke up early in the morning when the train stopped at a station named Dhopakandi. Helaluddin had heard of this station from their father. He knew it was a port city with a train station and river ports. His father used to tell him about a friend who lived here. Sirajuddin was a very well-known tradesman of this town, and his father always visited him every time he came here. Helaluddin decided to look for this person. He bought a few steamed rice balls from the street side vendor for breakfast. After almost a daylong search, they finally found a certain Sirajuddin who owned a retail clothing store. The gentleman took them in as his own children and asked them to live with him as a part of his family. But Helaluddin did not want that. He decided to accept his offer as a temporary solution and requested him to find a way to send the two of them to their own home in the village.

"You are too weak and stressed from all the troubles that you two went through," he said, "I'll surely find a way to send you back home. But until then, take a rest for a few days and stay as my guest."

Their village did not change much, except for the fact that most of the known faces had either left the village or died. Some had returned and tried to revive normalcy in a ghost village. They saw unattended gardens and untreated trees everywhere. The big Hijal tree stood alone, covered with all its dead flower clusters. They had spent so many days playing under this huge tree. Helaluddin remembered the ghost stories that people used to tell about this tree. He used to avoid the tree during evening times since the tree was supposed to house ghosts that wanted to return to their homes in the evenings, undisturbed. Helena was excited to come back to the village, just like her brother was. The happy excitement disappeared the moment they reached their house. It was not deserted anymore; some strangers occupied it and established a new household.

"This is Makbul Hossain Sarkar's house, and these are his children. Their parents were taken by Olabibi, and the orphans have come back to their home," Sirajuddin approached the head of the new household and introduced the original owners.

"But we have papers," said the man. He then brought a bunch of papers and showed them to Sirajuddin. Helaluddin sensed that something was terribly wrong. These people lived in that house as if they owned it. Women were busy inside, while children played happily in the courtyard. Something was definitely wrong.

"Your father's stepbrother has sold this house to them," Sirajuddin sighed. "It's not your house anymore. They have legal papers." This was not the only new family in the village; after the cholera epidemic, people were scared to come back and started selling their homes at cheap prices. Their Uncle had just taken the opportunity and sold this house to earn some easy cash. They did not have any right to the house they were told. The court document recorded their late grandfather's will in which he gave all his property to his other son in case of his firstborn's sudden demise. The grandchildren were not listed as rightful heirs.

"I will go to the courthouse to make sure these are not forged documents," Sirajuddin declared.

"Please let the children stay with us while you resolve the issue; after all, it is their house," the kind gentleman proposed.

Helaluddin slowly walked toward the window and saw his reading desk, full of someone else's books. The lamp was still there: a pretty little lamp that gave him light all those days. A lump of sadness clotted in his throat and Helaluddin gave out a howling cry. He cried for his dead father, and he called aloud his mother. He cried like a little lost child, trying to fathom the pain of loss and remembrance. Helena sat beside him and cried, asking nonstop, "Brother, what happened? What's wrong? Brother, what happened? What's wrong?"

Helaluddin pulled her by the hand and ran. He got into the bullock cart that brought them to the village. Sirajuddin ran after them and found the two sitting in the bullock cart.

Everything was gone. Olabibi took away his parents; an Uncle usurped them; strangers took over their lands. Was it the beginning of his urge to occupy lands? Did that feeling of loss engrave on his mind, the desire to gain more and more lands as a means of self-justification? Was he really greedy? Or was it that he wanted to dissolve the bitten, old, corrupted social structure and replace it with a new kind of harmony in his own way? Which one was real? Was it his greed, or was it the desire to build a new world around him? He was still unsure.

"Sometimes you wake up. Sometimes the fall kills you. And sometimes, when you fall, you fly."

— <u>Neil Gaiman</u>

Chapter 13
The Primordial Burden of Blood

Is there anything stranger than the human mind? How extraordinary is its ability to let events and incidents fall upon it, and reflect light and shadows beyond human grasp! A surge of endless color, this mind is. New shades and tints are born with every coating, every dilution of various colors. Everything waits at the tip of your brush, waiting for you to mix and create, with one brush stroke after another, empowered by your own mighty mind. Helaluddin still could not fathom the strength of his own will power. How, as a young boy, did he have that courage to stand up against all odds and turned back toward the light instead of jumping into the abyss of darkness?

"Find me a job, anything, and rent us a small room near your house. But please don't make us be your burden," Helaluddin told his benefactor. Sirajuddin had realized by that time the mental strength of that teen-ager and decided to help him grow stronger. He helped him get a job at the tollbooth by the river and rented a small one-bedroom house for the two siblings. It was arranged that Helena would spend his days with the Sirajuddin family and go back in the evening when Helaluddin returned from work. Sirajuddin's wife bought new kitchen utensils for this new family and taught Helena how to cook. One day, Helaluddin came home to find his sister waiting for him, to treat him with food that she had cooked herself: rice, Hilsa fish sautéed in Mustard paste, deep-fried small Puti fish, mashed eggs and potatoes seasoned with mustard oil and red chili powder. The two siblings took their meal together, like two happy children, forgetting all the pains and troubles around them. Helaluddin noticed Helena had real culinary skills; she was really a good cook and a great housekeeper. Life felt peaceful at times until Helena's nightmares disrupted that flow. Helena started seeing things. She became scared of nightmares and stopped sleeping through the nights. The moment Helaluddin went to bed to have a restful night, Helena's restlessness would start. She would start screaming or come running to Helaluddin's bed, shaken and terribly scared:

"Brother, there's a snake in my bed! Come look! There's a snake coiled in the middle of my bed!"

Helaluddin had to get up and light the lamp to check her bed.

"Where is it? Where? I don't see any snakes."

"But I do. I see snakes, and I see."

"What? What do you see?"

"I see Olabibi, clad in a white sari, roaming in the courtyard, sitting by my bedside. She talks to me. She sits with me all night and talks all night. She tells me things."

The rest of the night, Helena would not sleep. She would stay awake the whole night and talk gibberish. She would talk about things that were not there, not then, not ever. And she would guard her two eyes against closing.

Sleep would become the bearer of a nightmare for her for a few days after that. She would stay up all night and then sleep all day. Helaluddin had to lock her in the room when he went out in the morning.

Sirajuddin's wife did not believe in allopathic medicine, so she suggested that they brought the spiritual healer to cure her of her illness. Her other treatment option was to get Helaluddin married. His wife would be a good companion and help Helena get better soon, the benefactor's wife said. But Helaluddin was not sure about this idea of marriage. What if the new bride was too cruel or too indignant to tolerate Helena? Of course, the third option was to marry Helena off to a suitable young man. But who would marry a woman who saw things that were not there? There were a few proposals of marriage for Helena, and the groom's family ultimately backed off after finding out about Helena's condition, and that ended the possibility of a new future for her. Helaluddin was not worried though: he'd rather have Helena stay with him until she grew out of her illness. Helena ran her household quite like an expert, cooking, and cleaning and mastering her culinary talent, and Helaluddin kept himself busy working at the river toll booth, dreaming of a better future for himself and his sister.

Shamsher Shekh was a kind boss and an acute observer too. He took notice of Helaluddin the day he started working in the booth. He watched Helaluddin's management skill, his knack for bookkeeping, and knew that he could make good use of this new worker. A new island was formed by the south end of the river, and Shamsher Shekh had his eyes fixed on that new land. He called Helaluddin one day and told him to go there and take a detailed measurement of the area. He asked him to follow discretion regarding the project. No one must know why he was there, what he was doing, or whom he was working for. He should go there in the pretense of a fisherman or carry a basket as if to collect fresh and dry sand for cooking purposes. He had to measure the land and return without being noticed.

"Take a note of everything. How big is the land? How many entrances from the mainland? What is the condition of vegetation and the texture of soil or land? Observe everything and give me a comprehensive report. Will you be able to do it?"

"Yes, sir."

Helaluddin took with him a big clay pot, and walked around the newly formed land. He saw a few other people strolling there. Two cruel-looking men stood at the entrance almost like; the guards of the land and stopped him as he entered.

"Why are you here? What do you want?"

"My mother sent me," Helaluddin showed them his big earthen pot. "She needs a big pot of fresh and dry sand to pop her rice. She sells puffed rice, you see."

"Where do you live?"

"Just by the east side of the river and we don't get sand there. Our riverbank is muddy and murky."

"Okay. Fill your pot and run back home."

Helaluddin came back with a detailed report for Shamsher Shekh, and that was the beginning for him. The excitement, the fun, and the fear of locating a new land and measuring it, and then sending a band of strong men to fight for that land and then finally claiming that land as one's own! What a thrill! Shamsher Shekh's *Lathial* troops went in and fought with Nizam Molla's fighters and finally won the possession of that land. People were injured from both groups; a few died; then, arrived the police force to bring law and order. Lawyers were brought in by both sides for litigation and mitigation. And after everything, Shamsher Shekh was declared the legal claimant and possessor of the new land. That was just the start for him. Helaluddin landed a job as Shamsher Shekh's investigator for new lands. He would travel around the river and look for newly risen fertile river lands and investigate their condition. Based on his report, Shamsher Shekh would decide which lands to claim and which to discard. Hunting for unclaimed isles became his adventure, his obsession, his passion. Hunting for new isles for Shamsher Shekh was his means of survival, but he did not want to stop there. Was this the only river, and did new lands only pop up around this river? Why shouldn't he start a venture of his own and look for new lands to set up his own claim?

The village had a group of people with money and land, and another group that hankered after everything; the rest of the poor villagers fell under two categories: the needy and the needed. Greed, dishonesty, lying, and deception were a few means of survival techniques used by the needy ones. If they had their minimum requirements of livelihood met, these needy people would turn into honest working force. They needed groups, on the other hand, who would stand by you to guard you and give up their lives for you if you could justify your need and dependence on them. They would form fighting troop around you. Helaluddin decided to engage these two groups in his future plans of hunting and claiming new river lands far away from Shamsher

Shekh's territory. The plan might have taken a long time to come to light; he might have delayed the process to take a better preparation, if only—had he not—had the incident not—occurred in his life. That incident changed everything, making him realize his limitations—his sinful limitations, his failure to take control—and forcing him to leave everything behind and run away, like a hapless coward.

Days passed by, and time healed their wounds of loss and suffering. Years went by, like fickle wind, leaving two grown-up siblings to handle their grown-up days. Helaluddin was a strong, muscular young man, working hard all day long for Shamsher Shekh and making plans of procuring his own islands in his leisure time. Helena's mental condition had not improved at all. Helaluddin had brought in doctors from the neighboring cities to treat and cure Helena of her ailment, but no one seemed to have any solid diagnosis. It was a mental illness: the doctors concurred and prescribed a few medicines. They advised him to take her to the city general hospital for better treatment, but Helena did not want to go and Helaluddin did not force her. Helena's illness was not in a dangerous condition that would make people scared of her. She would just have these occasional bouts of frenzies when she would scream and curse at some invisible enemies and throw at them anything that came to her reach—plates, cups, bricks. During such frenzies, the one woman who could pacify her was their benefactor's wife. The good woman would always stand by her side and convinced the villagers that Helena lost control over her emotions the night *Olabibi* took away her parents. Her memory of that night sometimes made her crazy. Villagers felt somewhat sympathetic to the orphan girl and eventually got used to her occasional hysteric fits. As she grew older, Helena's condition worsened, and it at times became difficult for Helaluddin to manage.

That night Shamsher Shekh was in a happy mood. He made a good profit and wanted to celebrate the night with his hardworking employees. Shamsher Shekh invited Helaluddin and others to join him for a celebratory dinner: Mutton, rice, liquor. Helaluddin did not drink. When he was young, he had seen his father take a few drinks of some reddish liquor diluted with water. He did not know what it was then. He knew now, but he still did not drink. He took a few bites of the curried mutton and took his leave. When he reached home, he saw Helena waiting to serve his dinner. She had cooked some fish and vegetable curry: dishes of parwal and Puti fish, cubed gourd, and shrimp, and masoor daal. She had set the table for two. The moment Helaluddin entered, Helena came running and hugged him tightly.

"You are here! Did you see that?"

"Yes, I did! You have cooked my favorite dishes. That's why I came back without dining with my boss. I had a feeling that you had cooked a delicious meal!"

"No, not the food! Look inside the curry bowl. Do you see?"

"What do you mean?"

"Look closely! The curry bowls are swarmed with maggots! Where did they come from?"

"Where do you see maggots? Nothing is here. Look, here. I am eating a few cubes of gourd from this bowl, and a piece of fish from this bowl. Look, there's nothing else. Yum, yum, Yummy! "

"No, no, they are full of maggots and larvae!"

"Ok, look at me, I am going to have a delectable dinner now because I see nothing wrong, nothing floating, nothing crawling in my food." Helaluddin sat to eat. But Helena did not join him. She sat in one corner and kept crying. "I have cooked my heart out here, and what do I see in the end? Bowls of crawling, creeping maggots. Where did they come from, Brother? Why are these maggots swimming in my curry?"

Helaluddin finished his dinner and put away the dishes. He then brought some dried-flattened rice and *Patali gur* for her, but she still did not eat. She spat every morsel out and kept screaming, "Look, look, the maggots! They are in here too! I bet Sirajuddin, Uncle's wife, had infested everything with these worms! I bet she hates me!" Helaluddin put Helena to bed. "Go to sleep; everything will be fine in the morning." He then turned off the lamp and went to bed, taking his worries with him.

"Are you sleeping Brother, are you awake? They are in my bed too! Come look, look, they are going to eat me out! They will get inside my head through my ears!" Helena was shaking like a bamboo leaf. Helaluddin brought her to his bed and wrapped his blanket around her and held her tight just so to make her shaking to stop.

But it did not stop—the shaking, the screaming, the frenzies, and fear. Helaluddin held her as tightly and as close as possible to himself as Helena kept talking about meaning things. She slept for a few seconds and woke up in utter horror, complaining about tiny worms crawling over her body. He dozed off for a moment and then startled back to reality as Helena trembled and cried and complained. Why did she suffer from a disease that he could not find a cure to? Why not a physical ailment? What had Helena done to deserve such a painful disintegration of sanity? If she suffered from fever or other illnesses, he could have had the ability to nurse him, but what could he do now? How could he help his sister get rid of her pains?

Helaluddin started crying. He held his sister with all his strength and watched the storm pass as she felt composed and slowly gave in to slumber. Helaluddin stroke her unruly hair and remembered those ominous days when the two of them sat like this for three days and three nights by the bedside of their dead parents. Helena was so little then. But now, he looked at the sleeping Helena and realized something strange had taken place in her. She was not a little girl anymore. He saw a grown-up woman lying comfortably by his chest, with her hair hanging loosely around her face, like storm withered bamboo leaves. Her body had grown as if it belonged to somebody else. Her breath—warm and peaceful—fell on his face and ignited in him a new feeling of warmth, a feeling that he did not think could be evoked by the rhythmic flow of a sister's exhaled breath. Helaluddin allowed his senses to go numb under the spell of that breathing rhythm of warmth and forgot his time, place, and civilization. Everything melted down, the whole world did, amidst that crux of a fading world, the only reality presented itself in the form of two human beings with their unbeatable survival instinct. For Helaluddin, the only truth lay on his power to save his sister and survive amidst all adversaries. The whole world was useless if he failed to comfort Helena and if he failed to beat all odds. Helena melted like a broken primordial element that had suddenly come in contact with the ultimate source of all power—the warmth of a manly fire. Like Adam and Eve, a man and a woman then sought shelter in each other's warmth in a world that defied all history.

"Pain is inevitable. Suffering is optional."

— <u>Haruki Murakami</u>

Chapter 14

The Umbrageous Soul of Mine!

In spring, the island began to show signs of fertile green, like a freshly grown beard of a dashingly handsome man. The land was ready to produce a good harvest that year. Every part of the island burst out of in fertile greeneries. Every piece of cultivable land showed off some new plants, various new crops, and the growing frenzy kept growing all around the island: Pigeon Peas, Mosoor, Urad, Garbanzo Beans grew abundant everywhere. You sit by the riverbank facing the island, and all you see is pure endless green patch after patch, and one unending green canvas. In between, Indian forage grass spreads sprinkles of white and gold stuck on top of long stems. The *Jiga* trees by the roadside were also in full bloom. The whole island got into this fertile festive mood, and the children added more rhythm to it by adding drumbeats. These children collected the stomach linings of slaughtered cows and stretched them to fit over a circular clay pot. As the lining dried, it became a strong drum that could produce the best and the crisp sound that one needed in order to give the harvesting season its best momentum. Children broke into little groups and performed their drum-beating ritual, from one house to another, generating the mood of feast and festivity.

Noor Mohammad always enjoyed these festive occasions; he would always join these drum bands and run around with them. He also liked to take care of his pet goats, Black and White—one had a fifty percent black blotch on its body, and the other, fifty percent white blotch. If he stood them side-by-side, they would complement each other as one monochromatic flow—pure black and pure white. Noor Mohammad, therefore, named them Black and White. He played with his new pets all day long and let them loose in the fields to graze. Within a month, his two goats became strong and plump, from having free access to all greens and beans of the island. The crops were ready for harvest, Noor Mohammad noticed. The paddy shafts were golden ripe, the peas and beans are fully grown—strong outside, but juicy inside. Noor Mohammad knew that his uncle would have to call for his hiring hands and those indentured workforces who worked for food and grains, and in return, helped his uncle reap and store his crops. The other farmers had already started the harvesting event by inviting the Moulavi to run special prayers in praise of Allah and his prophet. These prayer ceremonies, Quran recital events were always followed by a hearty feast. Noor Mohammad had accompanied his Arabic teacher, the Moulavi, of village Madrassa to a few of those celebratory feasts. His uncle's feast; was scheduled for the following Friday. All the hired hands would stay in their palm-thatched quarters outside the Courtyard and devour delectable breakfast, lunch, and dinner for a good number of days until the harvest was complete. Since the hired men were only paid: with food and grains, they were always given delectable feasts. Rice Pilaf, Chicken Korma, Beef Curry, Sweetened basmati rice cooked in milk and *patali gurh* were just a few of the dishes that they were served. It carried more, if not, almost the same flare of a wedding party. The poor hired hands shad hardly any other chance to feast on such rich and scrumptious food: they looked forward to the harvesting season all year long for this festive season and for the harvest feast thrown by his uncle. This year, his uncle's overabundant crop would require two phases of harvesting, which made the workers even more excited.

The workers started to gather in the courtyard after the Jumma prayer. They brought their own hookah and tobacco leaves and added water or molasses to soak the tobacco leaves for the desired taste. They snacked on a Wicker basket full of puffed rice and *patali gurh,* and smoked their hookah while Zayeda and other housemaids kept busy in the kitchen helping his mother prepare the harvest feast.

Zayeda always helped Helena in the kitchen, and she was also quite affectionate, and at times extra careful in her treatment of Helena. Helena always felt grateful and happy for having a friendly soul around.

"Sister, you look tired. Should I massage your feet or something?" Zayeda started giving her a foot massage without waiting for her response and continued her chitchat.

"How do you feel, Sister?"

"It feels so good! I really needed such a massage right now. Thank you for understanding!"

"No. I mean, how do you feel when you know."

"Oh, I don't know, I mean, I don't even seem to remember after the bout. People say I say things or do things, but I don't have any memory afterward. I wish I knew." Helena sighed.

"You poor soul," Zayeda whispered and kept massaging Helena's feet.

The workers got busy with their work the moment morning light broke. Happily, they gathered their harvesting tools and ran to the field, some of them sang on their way to the field:

By the evergreen and growing field of Rattan
Works all day the youthful young man
The man works and keeps complaining
"Dear Sister-in-Law, I am starving!
Feed me a bowl of water-soaked rice."
The feeble youth plows the land and keeps complaining
"Where's my breakfast, dear sister-in-law of mine?
A bowl of soaked rice, with some salt, red chili, and onion
Sister-in-Law, do serve me that rice. My stomach is growling!"

That morning, Noor Mohammad woke up to a festive day. He took his two cows for grazing by the riverbank. He brought with him a torch, a bottle of kerosene and, a matchbox. He stuck the bamboo torch in the ground, filled it with kerosene oil, and ignited the wick. Noor Mohammad then stepped back a few steps from the torch to check if it was completely lit. Then he slowly walked toward the river and embarked on his boat, where he sat down quietly, facing the torch.

The torch slowly spread an aura of flame. Noor Mohammad closed his eyes and tried to forget about his surroundings. Sounds started to fade, chaos diminished, the world around him vanished; the only audible sound was his air that his lungs were pumping, and gradually, even that sound went beyond his auditory sense; and all sounds slowly surrendered to a newly rising sound: the whishing sound of fire. Noor Mohammad opened his eyes and saw the protruding hands of fire, spreading. Multiplying and reaching for the sky with its gaping mouths, one, two, three, four, five, six, seven—seven cavernous flares, extending towards the sky as a manifestation of their unyielding existence. Astounded, Noor Mohammad closed his eyes again and resumed his meditation.

"Noor, what are you doing? Worshipping the Fire God?" The voice said.

No, no! I am not worshipping the Fire.

Noor Mohammad opened his eyes again, refuting every argument the voice was making. The voice that lived inside him and cast a dice of doubt on every action or reaction that Noor Mohammad perceived. He grabbed his head with his two hands and covered his two ears with his hands, and he pressed his eyes closed as tightly as he could. But the voice continued. Noor Mohammad opened his eyes again to watch the seven burning flames that twisted and melted like liquefied iron from some Blacksmith's forge, which was bulging and spreading and extending to clasp him. Was this the Fire God that Pundit Khagen used to talk about? The Fire God with seven flaming tongues? Was it going to devour him, asking his body to submit to its sacrificial altar?

The seven flaming tongues of fire extended and touched him. They burnt him, and then they transmitted their heat into his body. In an utter horror, Noor Mohammad watched how his own body transformed into seven flames, burning and extending to encompass the whole world around him. He gave out almost an inhuman shriek and jumped into the river to quench his body.

Noor Mohammad came back home like a normal person. He hid his bamboo torch and the kerosene container in a secret hiding place, and went to the kitchen to check on his mother.

"Why did you take a bath this early morning, son?" His mother asked. She was still busy cooking meals for temporary workers.

Noor Mohammad did not respond to her query. He went inside to change his wet clothes and then walked toward the farming lands.

The workers came back by dusk, carrying the day's harvest. They piled up the harvest on one side of the big courtyard and went to bathe in the river.

The workers sat on the palm leaf mattresses spread for them on the floor. They sat in two long parallel lines and eagerly waited to be served. The servers started bringing big baskets of foods and started serving. The appetizer was deep-fried fluffy roti served with sweetened cream of wheat. Next came pilaf, chicken korma, and beef curry. Sweetened rice, cooked with milk and date jaggery was served as dessert. Noor Mohammad had eaten already and decided to oversee the feast as the servers kept pouring item after item to the hungry plates. These temporary farming helpers hardly had any opportunities to have searched for a hearty meal. The only time they tasted beef curry was during the Korbani Eid. Noor Mohammad watched hundreds of starving stomachs sitting in parallel lines and competing with each other to fill their famished body at ravenous speed.

Moti Mia, one such worker, seemed to have gambled his life on such splurge. He did not say 'no' to any servings and did not stop consuming until he could not go on anymore. After finishing his third serving of a big bowl of dessert, Moti Mia's body revolted in a sudden surge and reverted all he took in. Moti Mia sat placidly in front of his plateful of vomit, and its splatter, amidst an angry crowd. There was an uproar of disgust, and repulsion and the workers swerved away as far as possible from him.

Oh prick, Why take more when can't handle?

Son of a gun totally wrecked the feast.

What a ruffian! He doesn't even know when he is full.

Moti Mia sat there, utterly shocked. What a loss? What a tremendous loss of such a tasty feast? He kept thinking!

Noor Mohammad ran to his uncle and started crying "Uncle Helal, please make them stop insulting the poor man Please ask them to be quiet!"

"Now, get up people if you are done. Stop bothering the poor man. It's just an accident. It might very easily be anyone of you who had the same accident, no? I'm sure he didn't do it on purpose, did he?"

The crowd broke away and went to take a seat by the veranda to enjoy a few puffs of tobacco from their hookah. Noor Mohammad also went in to be ready for bed. The feeling of sadness stayed with him all night long. He could not forget the look of shame and sadness of that face—a man who ate the best meal of his life like a happy glutton but could not contain it. He was almost asleep when Uncle Helal entered his room and sat by his bed.

"I know why you were sad today," Uncle said, tousling Noor Mohammad's hair gently. "You are not like others. You have a soft heart that feels what others don't, and you have a pair of keen eyes that see what others can't."

"Hmm," Noor Mohammad whispered.

"These people, these poverty-struck people, always struggling to survive, always selling their life's strength to buy a few morsels of food. And they are given such a chance where they have the freedom to eat as much as they can, their malnourished greed, takes over and they do what they did tonight. And the sad part is, they don't even understand each other to realize that they share the same pain, the same hunger, same troublesome struggle for survival. No one understands that, no one. But you did."

Noor Mohammad started crying.

Uncle Helal took him in his arm and said, "I pray that you'll make a happy and prosperous future for yourself, my son. My blessings are always with you, my son, always with you."

Noor Mohammad realized that his uncle was also weeping silently. He stayed close to his uncle and felt a sudden warmth, a flow of pride running through his veins. No man had ever claimed him as a son before, NO ONE.

"We have not yet arrived, but every point at which we stop requires a re-definition of our destination."

— <u>Ben Okri</u>

Chapter 15

New Life, New Dwelling

Sometimes some incidents occur that completely change life's perspectives. Some of those occurrences result from one's lack of control over the situations, and some, from the lack of self-control. But who can be blamed for those situations that constantly seem to test one's lack of control and boldly try to remind one of such limitations? And does every such event always have to be a part of his life? Helaluddin was pondering on such issues of destiny and life while sitting by the riverbank, one early morning.

"Here you are! I've been looking for you," Hobibar said. He sat beside him on the wooden bench and whispered the rest of his information. They had found a newly risen delta, but it was a bit far from here. You would have to take a long two-day boat journey through the coastal down-tide to the East. Helaluddin suddenly felt relieved. This was what he needed right now, a digression, an adventure for new land.

The next morning, he started for the new island. Hobibar was his only companion. He did not want to disclose his real purpose to Shamsher Sheikh or anyone else. Everyone was told that he was going to town to run some errands. The hardest part was facing Helena. How can he stand before him after what happened last night?

"I am going away for a few days," He faltered. "I want you to go stay with Uncle Sirajuddin's family until I return." He then forgot the whole awkwardness for a moment all of a sudden and pulled Helena toward him to kiss her on the forehead.

"Come back as soon as you can, brother," Helena did not lift her head. She stood there looking at the earth beneath her feet as Helaluddin left in search of an adventure.

The newly risen delta ignited in Helaluddin this indomitable possibility for freedom. Freedom, but from what and to what end? What sort of freedom was he seeking? Was it a desire to be free from all bondage and barriers? Freedom from all establishments—law, society, values, and restrictions? What was the purpose of these struggles for freedom when the end result would be nothing but a new set of rules and laws to establish the concepts of newly found liberty? Nothing would change actually, except for the layer, the mask that covers everything. Helaluddin lay down on the freshly formed ground that had risen from the womb of a river. The soil was moist and dark. Helaluddin took a handful of that mushy dirt and smelled the fresh possibility of a fertile future. The island is fertile and would surely give him two big annual crops. It was surrounded by a river, and the nearest village was about a few miles away. Cultivation would not take much toil, and establishing a new settlement would not be difficult. His experience told him that no one had their eyes set on this new piece of land yet, and no one had placed any sign of ownership anywhere. His heart was beating like a drum—

of war, charge, defeat, and claim! This new land could bring him a new beginning. But how would he disclose this to his employer, Shamsher Sheikh? How would Sheikh take the news that his new employee had already started his own venture to become a landowner? Helaluddin had to come up with a plan to convince Shamsher Sheikh, and he decided to resolve that issue later. Meanwhile, he arranged for a boatload of lathi-fighters to accompany him in is pursuit. Tota Mian was the leader of this troop. He gathered his best fighters and embarked on the boat in the dead of night. Helaluddin took with him all his savings and set sail in pursuit of his island.

Taking possession of the island was completed quite peacefully. There was no opposition to fight against it. Only a few landless people from nearby areas approached to resist, but they were not an organized group. All they wanted was a piece of land to build their own homes on the island. Helaluddin happily permitted them to set up their new homes. He ordered his men to start building a house for him. Someone came with news that buying an old house from the neighboring village and then transport the materials to rebuild would be cheaper. The rich Hindu families from the neighboring village were leaving for India, one by one. They were not feeling safe as a minority in this country. Helaluddin bought a house and all the furniture from a Hindu repatriating family from the neighboring village and transported everything by boat. The old house was given a new build within a day, and all old wooden beds, chairs, cupboards, and chest of drawers were properly arranged. The House was ready for him and

Helena. He had to go back to bring Helena on this new island and start a new life.

Among the old pieces of furniture that he bought from the Shaha family was a bitten old wooden wardrobe. It belonged to Shaha's late grandmother. "Take it for free," Shaha had told him. "The wardrobe is of no use to us, and it does not have any keys." The lock was engraved on the wooden piece, and there was no way one could open it without the keys, unless of course, one wanted to ax it open. It was too old and almost useless. So no one bothered to open it after the old woman passed away. "Take it, or give us whatever you can. Even if you don't want to buy it, take it anyway because it is too heavy for us to carry across the border." Helaluddin took it for Helena. He thought he could fix it and have the local wood smith take a look; he might be able to open the lock without breaking the beautiful chest. Helaluddin tried to open the built-in wooden padlock. He took a chisel and inserted it through the chipped off area right in the mid-center of the carved lock and pushed and twisted it inside, trying to get into the hinge of the lock. He failed to open it and broke a corner of the top in the process. He pushed open through the broken part of the wardrobe door and looked inside. He found a bunch of small drawers and a built-in vault with lock and keys in one part and a few shelves on the other side. The inside of the wardrobe was in pristine condition. As he was about to close it, he found a key, hidden inside, tied with the wardrobe door. He took the key and inserted it through the padlock of the vault. What he found inside the vault changed his life for good. The hidden wealth left in that vault by a dead grandmother of a repatriating Hindu family: brought him riches and provided him with the opportunity to be a landlord, to be a powerful owner of multiple islands.

Helaluddin had acted quickly after procuring the accidental wealth. He invested money in buying a few other islands, completed building his house on the new island, and went back to Sirajuddin's house to bring Helena to live with him in the newly built home.

Sirajuddin's wife seemed relieved to see Helaluddin coming back for his sister.

"I am glad you are here, Helaluddin! I don't know how to tell you, and I am not sure I can tell you who is responsible for this? But Helena is pregnant."

"What! How do you know?" The whole sky had collapsed over Helaluddin's head.

"I have given birth five times in my life, and as a mother of three living children, of course, I know a pregnant woman when I see one."

Helaluddin sat dumbfounded.

"Should I make an arrangement to get rid of it before it's too noticeable?"

"Oh, no, no! Please don't do that!"

This is where life always pushed him—to the brink—from where you are left with only two options: either jump or walk back. He decided to take Helena with him to his new home.

No matter what life offers him this time, he will not surrender; he will not allow a life form to get destroyed— eliminated. But what will society think? Will it ever understand society? Will it ever understand the depth and dimension love can undertake? Why should it be so difficult to earn a social tolerance, if not acceptance? Will it be the first time in human history to have a child born out of a miracle? Won't the same society believe in that same miracle that it had believed thousands of years ago? Will it be too absurd an idea to have a child born without a father? Wasn't Jesus a conception of miracle? Wasn't Mary the miraculous virgin mother? Then why can't Helena be one? If one mysterious conception was accepted as a miracle once, then why can't that happen again?

Within seven days after their arrival at the island, Helaluddin arranged for Helena's marriage with Majibar—a simple natured and honest looking man from a neighboring village. He paid such a handsome dowry, an amount beyond the groom's expectation, that the groom's family was overjoyed to have Helena in their family. "The money is all yours," he told Majibar, "do what you will with it, but make sure you take good care of my sister; make sure you never hurt or abuse her."

Helena's wedding endowed him with a conflicted departing gift that was wrapped in both loneliness and a sense of relief. He felt Helena's absence in his life, and yet, that absence was not as intolerable as Helena's constant presence was. He was relieved to have unloaded a burden. Helaluddin involved himself more in his work of hunting and procuring new riverine lands and made time in between to visit Helena in the neighboring village. Helena's mother-in-law seemed to be displeased and never missed an opportunity to exhibit her aversion against Helena. She would complain about Helena's mental condition and report how her son—Helena's husband—was afraid of his new wife. Helena had started seeing things the mother in law always complained. Every time Helaluddin visited Helena, the mother in law would send a bucket of complaints against Helena with him, which he had to compensate by sending back more money. But her last bucket of the complaint was too heavy for Helaluddin to bear.

"Tell me this, dear sir, it's hardly a month since my son married your sister. Then why does her body show the signs of a pregnancy that is at least three months old?"

"I am not sure what you are saying. Maybe she has gained too much."

"My son is a plain and simple man. He does not understand your complicated arrangements; I just want you to make sure my son lives comfortably, well beyond comfort," she brought a meaningful smile on her face.

Helaluddin said nothing to the old woman. He checked on his sister's health before leaving that house. He promised to provide Majibar with all the money he would need for his business venture.

Helena gave birth to a son in one late autumn. Helaluddin ran to the village of Randhunibari to see the new mother and her child. Helena was holding her newborn in her arms when he arrived there.

"Give him a name, brother. I want you to name him."

"Your son will be named Noor, Noor Mohammad." Helaluddin put the newborn close to his chest. Helena laughed, and Helaluddin's whole heartfelt with the warmth of a morning day seeing her happy. He came back home a happy man and devoted all his time to improve the condition of all those poor men who had set up a new establishment on his new island. The land had to be sorted out and divided; the cultivable land had to be utilized properly and should be given to farmers who would either buy or lease them from him. He also had to establish schools and mosques and other facilities for public benefit. He lost track of time as he kept himself busy in his island development project for months.

Then one morning, Helena came back. Helaluddin came home from work one day and found Helena sitting in his house, with her little baby on her lap. "They have sent me away," She said. "They don't want me or my kid in that house." Helaluddin went to see Majibar and his mother. "What is my sister's crime? Why have you sent her away from her house?"

"This is not her house anymore," the mother in law said. "She gave birth to a child in less than five months after her marriage with my son. Don't you think we know? Do you consider us blind? People of the village are saying things, and that is ruining our family's reputation. We will not keep a fallen woman and her son in our house."

Helaluddin looked at the old woman's face. "What an amazing woman you are!" He exclaimed. You didn't mind squeezing money all these months. "Now that your son is all set, you are ready to dispose of her."

Helena never went back to her husband. Helaluddin ordered to build an extension to his house to accommodate Helena and her son. He told everyone that his sister would be living with him from now on, and it should not be a topic of gossip or rumor. But it is human nature to gossip, and people of *Shonai Char* were no exception to it. Some people talked behind his back, and some talked in public, even in his presence. Salamat, an over-inquisitive young man of the village, once challenged Helaluddin's authority by asking about the disparity of time between Helena's wedding and the time of her son's birth. "Isn't it suspicious to have given birth to a fully-grown child in such a short notice?" Salamat ignited in Helaluddin such overwhelming anger that provoked him to beat Salamat almost to death. After the Salamat incident, people of the village became cautious and learned to never taunt Helaluddin with embarrassing questions regarding Helena.

Once the pregnancy issue subsided, Helena's mental issue became another topic of discussion in the village. Helena's sickness was indeed eating her up. She gave up her calm and kept seeing things that are not there. Helaluddin took her to the psychiatric facility in Pabna, where she received electric shock treatment. But nothing seemed to work on her. Helena's occasional insanity became an inevitable part of her daily life. There were days when she was normal, like any other woman, a happy sister, a proud mother, a woman in control of her head. And there were days when she would hear voices and see things and scream and cry and rattle the whole house as if the whole universe around her would stop existing if she did not rattle it with her screams. Helaluddin could not look at her anymore. The experience of one ominous night had changed his life forever. Looking at Helena's face was not easy anymore, and even harder was to look at any other woman. One night's spontaneous physical awakening seemed to have sucked the very source of desire from him. He felt no yearning for a woman's body anymore. Was it his shame? His guilt? A conscience born out of his perverted mind? Or was it a self-imposed path for liberation from all bonding?

Helaluddin did not know. All he knew was that the newly found island was his life. That every dust of that island was precious like gold. That every piece of the land is cultivable and could produce crops of gold for him. And that the little island, with its immense future hidden beneath the fertile soil and within the lively inhabitants was a complete world in itself. And it was he who owned that world.

"Nobody deserves your tears, but whoever deserves them will not make you cry."

– <u>Gabriel García Márquez</u>

Chapter 16

Of Land and Politics

Everyone gathered in the courtyard of Helaluddin's house, waiting with excitement, and in anticipation of witnessing something unforeseen. They sat, forming a circle around a chair on which stood a small rectangle-talking box. The box had the power to generate a human voice; it spoke to people, talked, and sang to them. Quite a few of these villagers had had the opportunity to see this box when they visited the city. But the rest had only heard of a box that talked. The little box was called a transistor. It was a box that transmitted information about a world that's far away from these dark villages. Helaluddin had recently bought the transistor with an intent to stay informed about, his country, about the political unrests that were erupting all over. He used to listen to the station that played Tagore songs; lately, he hadn't been able to listen to Tagore songs because the transistor did not transmit them anymore. He was told that the government had banned broadcasting any songs written by a Hindu. Why should music be branded with a religion? What purpose would it serve if they stopped playing Tagore songs? Since when music became representative of race, religion, caste, and class? How was it possible to segregate a Rabindranath Tagore, from a Lalan Fakir, or a Nazrul Islam from a Tagore? Helaluddin did not have the answers to these questions that had been haunting him since the government banned the Tagore songs.

It was Sanwar the Attorney who first suggested to him that he should buy a transistor. "You'd be politically conscious and will stay connected with the world around you if you buy a transistor," Attorney Sanwar had told him. The world around him, was in fact changing, and that Helaluddin should start having some grasp over the changing world. It was not that he did not have any ideas about politics that ran in and over his country. He was aware of the political history of his subcontinent: he knew about the British rule and its ending; he knew about the birth of two new countries after the British left; he had seen the war between Pakistan and India, and now he was witnessing growing unrest between the two parts of Pakistan provoked by the disparately suppressive ruling policy that West Pakistan was implementing on the East. "But there's no end to knowing," Attorney Sanwar had said. "A transistor will give you news updates, and it will help you stay connected with the world and with your own people. You can let them gather at your house and listen to music, and you can let them hear the news broadcasted frequently. Your villagers will also know of the impending political turmoil of the country."

Helaluddin started inviting the villagers for a friendly gathering in his yard every night, where they would smoke their hookah and listen to the transistor and share their views about things they heard on the radio.

Attorney Sanwar had asked him to arrange for a meeting in his courtyard where he would give a talk about the current political situation of the country. Helaluddin called for a meeting to be held after Jumma on a Friday. The news of this meeting was announced in the village so that people could make time to attend. Sanwar was scheduled to go to Rajapur to deliver another speech, and Helaluddin was also expected to join him.

Sanwar arrived on time. He wore white tunic and pantaloons and a Cashmere shawl nicely placed on his shoulder. When Sanwar stood on the podium to deliver his speech, Helaluddin was impressed with his charismatic leadership. Attorney Sanwar knew how to talk in public; he knew how to get people's attention and how to easily explain the most complicated things; he knew how to spread knowledge among the ignorant ones without offending anyone. Sanwar explained the internal politics that created a divide between Countries called Pakistan; he explained how West Pakistan economically oppressed the East and was milking the East only to build a beautiful west side of the same country. East Pakistan was treated like a colony and nothing else, he said. Sanwar talked about the language movement of 1952—the movement that sowed the seed of the impending liberation movement. Sanwar explained in detail the six-phase declaration of autonomy that Sheikh Mujib had proposed and the punishment that was imposed on Sheikh Mujib for making that proposition. It was about time for the people of East Pakistan to ask West Pakistan to treat them equally and give them their rights to enjoy everything on equal grounds.

"Mr. Attorney, why will they deprive us of our rights, being our Muslim brothers?" An inquisitive villager asked. He could not believe that the West Pakistanis would not show respect to their East Pakistani Muslim brothers.

"Just because we share the same religion with the oppressors doesn't make them a lesser oppressor. Religion has nothing to do with this kind of politics. Do you remember the proposal to build the Yamuna Bridge that was passed in 1966? Have you seen that proposal in action? Do you see a bridge over the Yamuna River? Have they even started building one?"

"No, I don't see any bridge or any construction of that bridge in the process."

"My point, precisely! You will not see it because it will not happen. They will not make it to give us easy transportation for our goods and products. They want to make money by buying things that we produce on the Eastside and then rebranding and reselling the same goods for more money. They make profits over our own products."

"All these six-phase autonomy proposals are nothing but a conspiracy being implemented by the neighboring Hindu country," the Moulavi, of the mosque remarked.

"Read the six-demands that Sheikh Mujib is making. Read them closely. Is he saying anywhere that we want to go back and become a province of India? I don't think so. Then why are you calling it a Hindu conspiracy? All it talks about is our rights and rightful dues that West Pakistan is depriving us of, and you are using the shield of religion to deny the oppression and defy our rights? An election is coming, and I want every one of you to be conscious of your voting rights. Be cautious, be conscious, be aware, and be the watch guard of your own rights as a citizen."

Sanwar concluded his speech and sat down, watching people's reactions. Some said he was speaking the truth; some said they were mere ginger merchants in this big world of business and had no interest in knowing the business of the big ships; some called it a day, leaving the responsibility to stir a movement for someone else. Sanwar, however, did not expect these people to get instantly involved in the movement; he just wanted them to start thinking and that they had started. These ignorant people had started thinking about their rights. Once the thinking mind is awakened, a revolution would not be difficult, but it is the power of radicalism that bothered him. People would surely use religion as a vehicle to control these ignorant and God-fearing minds. Sanwar was aware of Abdul Matin of the Muslim League, a cunning man who was using religion as his tool to confuse and control the mob. Abdul Matin was speaking at a public gathering in favor of Pakistan, blaming the Hindus of India for creating havoc in the country and calling Sheikh Mujib a spy of India. Poor ignorant villagers will happily concede when religion is a weapon. No one will believe anything against the Muslim brotherhood. But Sanwar had faith in people that one day they will rise to claim and protect their rights.

The public gathering of Rajapur Bazaar was a tremendous success. People joined by thousands and paid attention to what Sanwar had to say. Helaluddin had appointed volunteers to keep watchful eyes over the venue. He had asked them to report the moment they saw any spy from Abdul Matin's political party. Reports came about the presence of Abdul Matin's people, surveying, and watching people's reactions. Helaluddin was also anxious to know about the activity of another man: Mojnu from the village Betil. He had information about Mojnu's secret plans to seize *Isle Sonai.*

Mojnu would attack any day, he was told. He had to be on the watch and always prepared. Helaluddin spent his days staying in touch—with the turbulent political events of the country through his tiny transistor, and with the secret plans of attack, which Mojnu might initiate on him any day. He had to be prepared for everything.

Sirajuddin had written a letter. Helaluddin had won the lawsuit he had filed against his Step-Uncle; Helena and Helaluddin had earned back their right to their property, Sirajuddin wrote. His health had deteriorated since Helaluddin saw him last time. Before starting for a journey toward the afterlife, Sirajuddin wanted to make sure he kept the promise that he had once made to a young boy named Helaluddin, who came and asked for his help. Helaluddin's heart filled with affection for this gentleman. A stranger, and yet more than a family, Sirajuddin had kept his promise and had done what a father would do for his children. Helaluddin folded the letter and put it back in his pocket. He also had to complete a few unfinished tasks before death would take away all his time.

"In a way being loved is like being told you never have to die."

— <u>Timothy Findley</u>

Chapter 17

The Ordinary and Beyond

Pundit Khagen decided to test the range of Noor Mohammad's knowledge of Math, Bengali, History, and Science. He had been home tutoring Noor Mohammad for a while now, and it was time that he tested his student's aptitude. Noor Mohammad passed all his tests with flying colors and made his tutor extremely proud. But Noor Mohammad's unstable headache prevented him from sharing that feeling of pride; after taking the hours-long aptitude tests, the spark of intermittent pain in his head took control over his body and trapped him in a cage of gloom. He liked walking by the river and cool his head off whenever he was attacked by any such bout of headaches. But the doctor had advised Uncle Helaluddin to keep him under supervision; Noor Mohammad, therefore, was never left alone in his current physical state. Whenever his head was taken over by such overwhelming confusion and pains, Noor Mohammad always wanted to go light his bamboo torch; he knew the lighted bamboo torch would instantly make him feel better. He knew all he needed was to sit by the river with a lit bamboo torch by his side. But everyone was guarding him, and he saw no chance to escape. He was grounded for eternity.

"Let's go by the river, why aren't you going there? Let's go?" The voice kept asking him.

"I can't."

"I'm telling you, we should leave the house at once and go sit by the river."

"I can't, because Uncle Helaluddin has forbidden me to go."

"We must go now. We must go and light the torch."

"I can't go. I can't take the torch out from its secret hiding place. Everyone will see it. Everyone will know."

"But we must go light the fire," kept saying the voice, "we must light it because that's what your Uncle doesn't want you to do—he is trying to take you away from your fire. He wants you to forget about your fire."

"Why should my uncle do that? What's in it for him?"

"Everything! He is dividing you. He is breaking your union with your fire. You and your fire are one, indivisible entity. The fire is you; you are the fire."

"Who are you talking to, Noor Mohammad?" Helaluddin walked in and asked.

"Nobody, Uncle. I am not talking to anyone."

Helaluddin frowned; he was sure he had heard Noor Mohammad talking to some invisible person; someone was trying to convince him to do something and Noor Mohammad was trying to evade. *This was not a good sign,* he thought. Helena started with the same symptoms. Was Noor Mohammad going to inherit Helena's condition? Helaluddin decided to take Noor Mohammad and Helena to be checked out in the psychiatric facility in Pabna, where he once had brought Helena to get her treatment. Noor Mohammad had been a recluse for some weeks by then and had stopped eating or communicating with anyone. All he did was talk to himself, arguing with some invisible companion.

Noor Mohammad did not object when his uncle took him and his mother for a visit to the hospital in Pabna. They took a rickshaw to the train station and got on board to a train to reach Iswardi. From Iswardi, they had to take an hour-long bus ride before they reached their destination. Helaluddin rented a hotel for the night. Noor Mohammad stayed quiet during the whole journey and stayed as quiet when they visited the doctor the next day. The doctor, a young psychiatrist, spoke with Noor Mohammad in private and spent extra time with Helaluddin and Helena in his effort to understand Noor Mohammad. After the initial examination, he admitted Noor Mohammad to the hospital and asked Helaluddin to come back after a week. Helena also had to be admitted to receive her electric shock treatment. Helaluddin left the mother and her son in the hospital compound and came back to his hotel room with a heavy heart. This was one thing that he always feared—that Helena and Noor sharing the same symptoms—and this was the only thing he never wanted to happen, and yet it had already happened, and he had nothing in his power to prevent it.

"He has inherited his mother's condition," the doctor told him when he went back after a week.

"Will he be okay? Is the condition too serious?"

"Well, not really; he's been detected before it was too late; he is quite young, and the treatment for this condition is also improved now, so it will be easy to treat and manage his condition."

"Just these medicines? Nothing else?"

"Yes, make sure he doesn't skip any dose, and make sure he is not under any stress or mental pressure. He is not going to handle mental stress well; also, let him mix with his friends and inspire him to be social and be around people. Be discreet about his condition for people might not react to it normally, which in turn will affect him."

Noor Mohammad heard everything. He looked sad and depressed, but he said nothing. The family came back to their village and resumed a normal life. Helena was feeling better, and Noor Mohammad was normal again, talking, laughing, and playing with his friends. Helaluddin's household was back to normal. But the village had gone through some turbulent time during their absence.

Abdul Matin had a political gathering in Rajapur Bazaar as a counteraction against Sanwar's event. Abdul Matin was giving his speech defending the goodwill of the ruling government when some people from the crowd burst into loud slogans in support of Sheikh Mujib, demanding the renunciation of the Agarhtala conspiracy case against Sheikh Mujib. The crowd divided into two groups—one in support of Sanwar's ideology and the other fraction supporting Abdul Matin—and broke into a fight. Mojnu, from the Village Betil, had brought with him an organized group of his own in support of Abdul Matin and allowed his armed group to attack the mob. Abdul Matin was a powerful man who owned factories and mills and had a strong connection with Pakistani retailers. A good number of villagers worked in his factories. Mojnu, on the other hand, was a rising landlord of the southern region; he had been planning for a while to extend his property and claim some more lands in this region. If only he could put his claim over Helaluddin's lands, he would become the richest landlord in that area.

Helaluddin decided to pay Sanwar a visit as he realized he also had to do something to break Mojnu's power. Helaluddin felt a sudden rush in his blood, the kind of rush that he usually felt when he ran in search of unclaimed cultivable lands. He felt intoxicated from the blood rush; he realized he was craving this excitement.

Attorney Sanwar handed him a list of secret allies. Young people around his village were actively involved in the uprising movement for liberation Sanwar had told him. He told him to take necessary precautions before contacting any of the people on the list, and he should always be prepared to help. The village was changing. People were changing. No one sat quietly anymore, only to listen to songs broadcasted on the radio. They talked, and they wanted to know. They knew—about events happening all around the country. No news stayed locally trapped anymore; if some political unrest happened in Dhaka, they knew; if the people of Dhaka protested against the Ayub regime, people of *Isle Sonai* expressed solidarity with the protestors the moment they came to know; the distance between the protestors in Dhaka and oppressed victims of a faraway village elapsed as information was not that unattainable anymore. Helaluddin had a transistor that transmitted news for everyone; Helaluddin's village was full of brave youth who were actively involved in generating information. Pakistan army had attacked the protestors in Dhaka and killed a brave rebel named Asaduzzaman. The villagers of Isle Sonai mourned the death and prayed for the martyr.

Military trucks started arriving in the village; the Government had declared Martial Law in the country and was adamant to demolish all miscreants to the dust, as they declared. People were afraid to come out; stores remained closed; the whole village became deserted because no one came outside. Helaluddin's evening gatherings were dismantled, and his transistor lost its usual position as the center of attention of an eager crowd. Helaluddin was scared to turn the volume on his radio when he listened to the news station. He would have to put the transistor by his ear and let it whisper to him.

One such night, when Helaluddin's transistor was whispering news to his ear, another voice whispered at him from outside.

"Mr. Talukdar, are you awake?"

Helaluddin took a torchlight and opened the window to check.

"Don't be afraid, Mr. Talukdar, open the door."

Three or four people jumped inside the moment Helaluddin opened the door. "Who are you?" He asked, "What do you want from me?" They had covered their bodies under big shawls and carried firearms under that cover. Helaluddin faltered a little but did not express any fear.

"What do you want?"

"Can you give us shelter for a few days? We need a hiding place for some days, and we need food. Can you arrange for our food and lodging?"

"But what if the Army comes looking for you?"

"They won't come to this area, but even if they do, we know how to tackle them."

Helaluddin still hesitated.

"Why are you asking so many questions? Either give us shelter or go to hell!"

"No, no, you don't have to kill me! I will help you anyway! Stay here, eat, sleep, and take a rest. But please be sure not to put me in danger. I don't want any Army invasion in my house."

"We are twelve people. Be discreet about your arrangement. No one should be aware of our presence."

Helaluddin went to Helena's room and woke her up. Zayeda also woke up and went to the kitchen to assist Helena. Ghota Mian went outside in the chicken coop and brought out a few hens and roosters to be used for dinner. Zayeda cooked a big pot of rice while Helena prepared the chicken curry. The leader of the group, Lutfar, signaled his men to come in for dinner once the food was ready. He asked two of them to guard the house while ten hungry people jumped over the food. The sudden commotion in the house had already awakened everyone up, and Noor Mohammad was also not an exception. He woke up to see twelve ghostly men inside their house, holding Sten guns and walking to and fro, eating food, and whispering to each other. Helaluddin asked his servants to make sleeping arrangements for his nocturnal guests in his spacious guest quarter. Twelve of them took turns sleeping and guarding the house. Noor Mohammad could not sleep, and neither could Helaluddin. He had given shelter to twelve armed men who were carrying firearms that he hadn't seen in his lifetime. He sat in his bed, waiting for the night to end. But the group decided to stay with them for two whole days, eating, sleeping, and guarding. On the third night, they informed Helaluddin that they were leaving after dinner. "You have done us a tremendous favor by allowing us to stay in your house, Mr. Talukdar," said Lutfar, the leader. "We are communist and ideologically, you belong to our enemy class, but still we came to you for help, because we are aware of your history—you know, of helping the poor, standing by the needy and helping them to stand up on their feet—and because of that reputation of yours, we considered you our ally. We were in desperate need of food and shelter, and you provided that for us. And for that we, are grateful."

Helaluddin said nothing, and the group leader continued:

"Since we have our moles all over the village and since we navigate in the secret hours of the night, we have to keep our ears and eyes open as we retain information, of all kinds, about everything. And we have information from a valid source that you are going be in the path of danger any day now; you should be careful, and you must keep some firearms for your own protection. Take this gun and this box of cartridges with you. You will need them."

"Thank you, but please don't leave any of those illegal firearms in my compound; I don't want to be in trouble with the police. If I need, I will buy a firearm and have it licensed."

"If you say so, but I was making a sincere offer. You should really be careful."

Lutfar and his group left. Helaluddin and Ghota Mia sat in the open courtyard, and Noor Mohammad sat with them as well—everyone trying to understand the dangerous excitement that they had confronted during the past few days.

"Lutfar seems like an educated guy," Helaluddin said.

"Yes, but his name isn't Lutfar though." Noor Mohammad remarked, "His real name is Arun."

"How do you know?"

"He told me."

"What? When?"

"Well, you were busy, making arrangements for their stay. They asked me to help them, so I drew a few posters and placards for them."

"I see."

"Uncle, Arun has a Master's degree. He has given me a book and has asked me to read it thoroughly."

"What book? Let me see."

Noor Mohammad brought out a book, a small fat book with a red cover, a book on revolution written by Mao Tse Tung.

"Burn it! You shouldn't be found owning a book on communism. Burn the book right now!" Helaluddin ordered.

"But please let me read it first. It won't take me long to finish it. I promise I'll burn it right after I am done."

Helaluddin gave in to the boy's request and asked him to go to bed. Everyone had been sleep-deprived for the past few days and must not get sick because of it, he said. Helaluddin stayed awake in his bed thinking about Arun, his ideology, and the secret information that Arun shared with him. Helaluddin knew time was geared toward a dangerous direction, and it was pulling him along. Other people of the village had also been trying to warn him of an impending danger.

In his dream, Helaluddin saw boatman Gauri again. Gauri was rowing his boat in a turbulent river and was going against a violent wind, and as he rowed his boat amidst the dangerous weather, Gauri, the boatman kept screaming as if to warn him: "Hey brother, watch out! Watch out, my brother!" Helaluddin woke up and felt out of breath. He had to do something, he told himself. He had to buy a gun for his protection; he had to protect his family; he had to tell Noor Mohammad, about this dream, about all dreams that the future might bring and past had bestowed on them. Helaluddin decided to tell Noor Mohammad everything about the dream, life, Truth. There was no point for Noor Mohammad not to know; after all, Noor Mohammad was nothing if he was not a part of Helaluddin.

"Then she cried without tears, which is said to hurt even more like dry labor."

— <u>Laura Esquivel</u>

Chapter 18
The Vanishing of Bindubashini

The morning started with its usual rhythm, with Ghota Mia raking the dried-out legume stems from the field and Helaluddin smoking his hookah and watching Ghota Mia work. Farmers passed by and asked Ghota for a share of dried legume hay to be used as fodder, but he was adamant not to give away anything for free. Helaluddin basked in the sun and enjoyed watching the flow of regular life around him. The flow was interrupted when Zayeda called him inside the house. "We have some visitors who want to talk to you," she said. Helaluddin followed her in the courtyard and saw Helena sitting with Bindubashini; Pundit Khagen was also there, with a look of inexplicable fear stamped on his face.

"Help me, dear Brother, please help me!" Bindubashini prostrated before Helaluddin and kept wailing, "O, Brother, please help me!"

"What happened? Why are you crying like this?' Helaluddin was quite taken by her sudden outburst.

"She is too shocked to say anything else, so let me explain," Pundit Khagen interrupted, "Montaz Shekh's older son has abducted Sushila, Bindubashini's older daughter, and has married her against her wishes. What is worse, they forcefully converted her to Islam and put her in isolation. Bindubashini has tried to talk to the perpetrators asking them to let her Daughter go, but that was of no avail. Her younger daughter became scared for her own life after the incident and eloped with Narendra, fearing they might come for her and convert her religion or violate her."

"I have nothing, nothing left, Mr. Talukdar," Bindubashini said. "My daughters are gone, my peace abducted, my religious rights violated in my own country. I have nothing else to lose."

Helena tried consoling Bindubashini and took her inside the house and made her eat something. As a devout Hindu, Bindubashini would normally refuse to eat in a Muslim household, but today she did not object.

Pundit Khagen sat like a broken tree. Helaluddin had no words to console these people; he was familiar with this pain of loss—the pain of watching others take over your house, your life, your very being, and then throw you away like a discarded shell. He had gone through such pains in his childhood. He had lost his home and his parents; he had been thrown into the wilderness of sufferings. He knew the ache and the agony of not belonging. When someone tries to pull away from the soil beneath your feet, there is no power strong enough in this earth to make you feel at home in that spiral of an abyss.

Helaluddin decided to pay Montaz Shekh a visit. He took Tota Mia and Surat Ali as his bodyguards. Montaz Shekh lived in Rajapur, a village not far from his territory. He remembered coming here to buy the old furniture and house from the Shaha family. People were nice then. They nodded at each other, and they stopped to greet the passers-by with a warm smile. The village had a feeling of warmth everywhere, with music and bells resonating in the temples and mirth and laughter filling the air. He used to come here to attend various cultural festivities and prayer rituals arranged by the Hindu community of that village. But today, the whole village looked deserted; most of the Hindu houses were either empty or repossessed by Muslim families; the familiar Hindu faces of that village seemed to have disappeared into thin air. What a dismal feeling of abandonment! What a bleak air of desertion and oppression! Despondently he walked towards the house of a man whose son had robbed a woman of her meaningful existence.

"Why have you come to our house, surrounded by bodyguards? Why have you brought your lathi fighters?" Montaz Shekh's older son challenged Helaluddin as Helaluddin entered their courtyard and asked for permission to speak with the head of that household.

"Show respect to your elders!" Montaz Shekh reprimanded his son and invited Helaluddin in.

"What can I do for you, Mr. Talukdar?" He asked.

"Nothing much; I just came to find out some truth. Is it true that your older son has kidnapped Sushila and forced her to change her religion? Is it true that he married her against her will?"

"You have been misinformed, Mr. Talukdar. My son did no such thing. She came here on her own accord. Besides, don't you know how rewarding it is for a Muslim if he can convert a non-believer into a believer? My son has done just that as a true Muslim."

Helaluddin still looked unsatisfied with the explanation.

"Can someone bring our new bride here?" Montaz Shekh asked his wife.

Mrs. Shekh brought in with her the new bride, clad in a new sari, with her face hidden behind the veil of her sari. Helaluddin could not see Sushila's face, but he watched her body tremble vigorously. He knew she was crying. "Are you okay, my child?" He asked. "Are you okay?"

Sushila burst into tears and started wailing loudly.

"Her name is not Sushila anymore, Mr. Talukdar," Montaz Shekh informed him. "She has been renamed as Mosammat Ayesha Khatun. She is a Muslim now. We all should call her by her Muslim name."

There was nothing he could do, nothing! The poor woman's fate was sealed.

"Your mother is worried about you. Do you want to convey any messages to her?"

"How is my mother doing, Uncle? O, dear, God! I hope my mother has the strength to bear this pain! Please tell her to forget me. Tell her that her daughter does not exist anymore." The woman wailed and groaned in utter agony as she was being taken away from the room.

"You have done a bad thing here, Montaz Shekh, a very bad thing! You shouldn't have allowed this in your house." Helaluddin grunted as he left the house. He realized the limitation of his power; everything was going through a rapid change; everyone is changing. Some were going with Attorney Sanwar's view, while others followed the views of Abdul Matin and Mojnu from the village Betil. Montaz Shekh and his sons were following the latter. They had established a business partnership with Matin, and they were being drawn to this new temptation of power.

Helaluddin felt powerless amidst that commanding surge of oppression. He had no news of hope to deliver to a destitute mother.

Pundit Khagen came to see him the next morning. Bindubashini had killed herself. Neighbors had found her lifeless body hanging like a withered leaf in a big custard apple tree. Pundit Khagen started crying like a little child. He embraced Noor Mohammad and kissed his forehead affectionately. "I cannot stay here in this country like this," He said. "Mr. Talukdar, this country is not for me anymore. I am going to leave this life behind in search of a new country in the neighboring one. I will go to India, Mr. Talukdar. I wish I could stay here and help Noor Mohammad with his studies, but that cannot be. I have made up my mind. Please make sure he gets a proper education. I've never seen a brilliant boy like him in my life, never."

The old man who had been a glorious teacher and a devout fighter of knowledge all his life took his leave from his motherland like one defeated soldier.

"…sometimes a start is all we ever get."

– <u>Junot Díaz</u>

Chapter 19

The Abysmal Anguish: Of Water,
Fire, and Departure

What is this feeling, this pain inside him, tormenting him, burning him like an incessant fire? What is it that burns him? What is it that felt the pain and yet stayed numb? What is this immense surge of power inside him that fails to be contained in words and language an expression? Is it in his soul? Is it his being, his very existence? Noor Mohammad was puzzled. He felt helpless and confounded by such an overwhelming surge of emotion. Was that how the human soul grew? Was this how each painful encounter imprinted a mark of experience on human life? Was he growing up? Was he losing touch with innocence? Was it how one felt when someone dear to one's soul got eradicated, uprooted, and thrown away? He wanted to scream as loudly as he could to let the world know that he did not want Pundit Khagen gone. His heart bled, feeling the pain of that suffering man, but yet he had nothing in his power to retain that man. The old man dragged his lifeless body with him, leaving his soul behind in a land that did not want him. Who decided that fate? Who was the one to decide who should go and who should live? How could one be sure that the ones that stayed were the ones that should stay? Who, if not Pundit Khagen had the right to stand on the soil that he had purified: by igniting the fire of knowledge, by spreading the light, the sparks, and the warmth of the Fire God? Why should a man like Pundit Khagen leave his homeland like this? Didn't he have the same right over the sky that hung over everyone's head, and the air they all of them breathed, and the soil that all of them tilled, and the sun and the moon and the starts that everyone viewed? To whom did this world belong? Who could claim possession over the land that so easily ejected her sons?

Noor Mohammad saw the disappearing feeble body of his teacher, a man whose heart contained the strength of a mountain. He did not recognize his surroundings anymore. The trees and the houses, the river and its shiny shore, and the chirping birds and the murmuring wind—everything looked fearfully strange to him. He ran out of the house and went in the direction of the river, He jumped into the river and swam for hours.

Noor Mohammad became a new person. He was forced to acknowledge the change—in him, around him and in everybody. Uncle Helaluddin was also a changed man. After Pundit Khagen had left for India, Uncle Helaluddin started spending most of his afternoon hours with Noor Mohammad. Uncle started giving him lessons: on history, country, and politics. He had a lot of things to teach him, Uncle had said. He had to prepare Noor Mohammad for the future. Noor Mohammad should be conscious of the political change that the country was undergoing. Uncle Helaluddin had told him about the country's past as well:

that the country was once ruled by the British for centuries; that British used traitors like Mojnu and Abdul Matin in their effort to establish their authority of the subcontinent and then gradually kept control over the country for hundreds of years; that after the *Swaraj* movement and against the growing uprising for liberation, the British realized their days of control were over and they left the subcontinent; but before leaving, they whimsically drew lines between lands and marked some territories as lands of dispute; that the British observed the birth of two different countries and left East Pakistan to dangle like a provincial state of Pakistan; and that the new political unrest was moving towards the formation of a new country. Uncle Helaluddin was a self-taught man. He used the story of his life as an analogy.

"I was born in a rich family and then was thrown into the street like a beggar. I had to live under people's oppression and pity. I needed my freedom, just like our country needs her freedom. I needed to build my own home, and so does a nation."

"But why are you connecting your life with this politics?"

"It's the same struggle—this desire for individual freedom for me and the nation's desire for freedom—they are the same. Sheikh Mujib has given this land a new name, Bangladesh. There will be a parliamentary election soon, and I am sure that very soon we will have a new country, a new and sovereign country, not a provincial state of Pakistan. I pray to God that I live longer to see the birth of that new country."

Noor Mohammad understood the analogy. The story of Uncle Helaluddin's struggle for freedom became analogous to the new struggle that he might have to go through, just so that he could claim his rightful possession over a new country. Uncle Helaluddin had his *Isle Sonai* to claim, and he, a new country.

Uncle Helaluddin cried like a little child after hearing the news of Sirajuddin's death. Noor Mohammad did not remember meeting that man for whom his uncle shed tears. But he knew how important that man was in his uncle's life. The old man had helped Uncle reclaim his property, which he had once lost. Now all the lands and all property that Uncle Helaluddin had owned were transferred into Noor Mohammad's name. Noor Mohammad was instructed to contact Attorney Sanwar in case of Uncle's sudden demise. Noor Mohammad listened to everything his uncle had to say, but he was not sure why his uncle was rushing into telling him everything. Why was Uncle so afraid? Of what? Noor Mohammad felt helpless and lonely? He had not known a world without his uncle. When he sat on his boat, watching his reflection in the water, the face that he saw floating beside his own was always his uncle's. He grew under the guidance and protection of an Uncle who stood by him the way a big tree stood over its seedling, guarding it, protecting it. Never for a moment had he thought that he might lose this canopy of love and shelter that his uncle had spread over his head. He was not ready to let go of that tree yet. But the change that he saw around him was too drastic, and Noor Mohammad was having a hard time keeping pace with the changing world.

His headache came back. One morning, Noor Mohammad woke up with his numbing headache and came out of the house to catch a breath of fresh air. He quickly started walking toward the riverbank. The world around him looked strange; people looked strange; everyone who walked by him had a face that was stretched from one corner to the other, and every face that was stretched from one corner to the other whooshed and swished by him, whispering only one word, repetitively, "Warning!" Warning! Warning! The voice in his head spoke the same word in the voice of a thousand drums: Warning, Warning, and Warning! The Voice spoke words of caution; it spoke words of knowledge—of history, math, science, the Quran. The Voice grew louder and louder as it kept reciting from the Quran, one chapter after another. Noor Mohammad pressed his two hands by his head and ran. And as he ran, he felt the whole village running after him; he saw everyone chasing him, cautioning him, screaming at him, "Noor, danger! Danger's on the way, Noor, danger is on the way!" Noor Mohammad ran for his Bamboo torch; he grabbed the torch and resumed running toward the riverbank. He lay down in the sand, putting the bamboo torch by his side. He closed his eyes and took a few deep breaths in an effort to gain control over the Voice in his head. He kept his eyes closed and did not stop breathing heavily until finally, the voice faded away. He opened his eyes and looked up in the sky and saw the white clouds in an autumn sky. He looked at the river and saw his tiny boat sitting quietly on a quiet river. Noor Mohammad slowly rose and took his Bamboo torch. He did not light his torch this time; he only carried it with him and got into his little dinghy. He sat on the platform of his dinghy in a prayer position and closed his eyes again as if he was praying his namaz. This was his favorite meditation posture. He could sit like this for hours and shut the outside world from his existence. He could recite the whole Quran from his memory and remember everything that he had read or learned in his life. He could concentrate within, forgetting about the world and its problems, the trees and their lives, the birds and their songs, the river and her waves, the sky and its empty winds. Everything gradually faded from his memories and his consciousness as Noor Mohammad sat there in prayer for a silence.

Everything went still for a moment, but then there was a sudden uproar. It was coming from the riverbank. Or was it emerging from within his head again? Are the voices coming back again? The cacophony of sound started resonating again: fluttering wings, chirping voice, rippling waves, rustling wind, and firecracker. Was that a firecracker? Or was it a sound of gunfire? One, two, three, four...more gunfire! A sudden panic took over Noor Mohammad's heart, and he rowed back to the shore and took his unlit bamboo torch and ran, this time toward his home.

People were running too, screaming, fighting, and running away from him, and with him, toward his house. He heard people: screaming, crying, moaning, and wailing. He recognized a few of the voices. As he reached the big Jackfruit tree in their front yard, he saw Asya and Zayeda rolling on the ground and crying. People stood in a circle, but not orbiting; people stood still in a circle. Noor Mohammad diffused that circle to go in and see what was within. He saw his mother's lifeless body holding in embrace another body that had no sign of life either—his uncle's body.

"My Parents, O, my parents!" Noor Mohammad jumped in and sprinted out. Zayeda came running after him and held him in a tight embrace. Noor Mohammad let his two eyes gush out with all their forces of uncontrollable sorrow.

There was a fight in *Isle Sonai* this morning. Tota and Surat Ali took their Lathi fighters there to resolve the dispute. Helaluddin did not accompany them this time. He decided to stay home and wait for his troops to come back after resolving the issue. He sat under the Jackfruit tree, enjoying his hookah. Three people suddenly emerged from nowhere and started shooting at him. The moment Helena heard the gunfire, she ran out and stood in front of her brother, trying to shield him with her body. The bullets struck her first and passed through her body, leaving both of them dead. Some said it was Mojnu, from the village Betil, who sent those hitmen; some said it was the Moulavi, of the *madrassa,* who worked as the spy for those goons; some said it was Abdul Matin, who had ordered the killing.

Noor Mohammad snatched himself away from Zayeda. He grabbed a match and lighted his Bamboo torch; with a burning torch in his hand, he then ran toward the place where the Moulavi lived, enjoying his unhindered privileges. Noor Mohammad sat outside the *madrassa* in his prayer posture. His headache was back again. The Voice was back; the voice spoke to him: "Look at the cruelty of this world!" The voice said, "Look!" Was he going crazy? Was he carrying in his blood the sign of his mother's insanity? But how can he be mad when so many other people who had heard such Voice were dubbed as something important? Why was he a madman for hearing the same voice that spreads beliefs to others? NO! He was not mad! He refused to define the voice inside his head as a sign of his insanity. Noor Mohammad stood up, holding the burning torch with his two hands. The flames grew stronger and stronger with every word of Pundit Khagen, which had stayed dormant inside his own head until now. And as he voiced the words that Pundit Khagen said, Noor Mohammad became the reincarnation of Pundit Khagen, of his every word, every spark of knowledge that he had ever uttered for Noor Mohammad.

Fire is the god of all gods. It is not the fire that you see or feel. It is the real face, the reincarnation of Mother Earth. The lightning in the sky, the scorching heat of the sun-god, the fuel hidden inside every tree—all these flow in a ceaseless stream of fire. The Fire God exists in everything in many forms. You find it within wood and timber, rocks and stones, and within the clouds. Friction gives birth to it. The Caveman chafed two stones together to initiate the birth of the Fire God, and civilization soon followed. Music plays its melodies in seven notes, the rainbow holds its colors in seven shades, and the Fire God represents itself in seven phases, through its seven flames. The Fire God arrives in two forms—in the form of a Creator and of a Destroyer. When He comes in his shape of a destroyer, he devours everything with his seven burning, flaming tongues and leaves behind only ashes and rubbles. And then He shines again, to cleanse and create and purify. The Fire God gives light and warmth and allows the new life forms to grow again.

Noor Mohammad stood there and watched the Fire God spread its strength everywhere, with its seven flaming tongues. It was purifying everything in its way: the Moulavi's house, the *madrassa*, and beyond. As Noor Mohammad stood there watching the purifying fury of the Fire God, he imagined himself as one of those seven flaming tongues.

"The mind was dreaming. The world was its dream."
> – <u>Jorge Luis Borges</u>

Chapter 20

In the End, Everything Begins

"Hey-ho! Watch out, Brother, be on your guard!" Boatman Gauri's high-pitched voice surpassed the gushing wind, the cascading rain, and the clamorous river. Words of caution vibrated like bellowing waves. Rain-drenched, he was standing by the riverbank. Sharp arrows of raindrops pierced the uncovered parts of his body: his face. Misty curtains of the incessant downpour blurred the distant village from his vision. Amidst the ceaseless water and the blustery wind, Gauri's little boat was only an inept necessity. With his strong muscular arm, Gauri sculled through the restless river, battling every wave with utmost mastery and yelling at the top of his voice, "Hey-ho! Watch out, Brother, be on your guard!"

The moment the boat reached near the shore, Gauri raised his oar and pushed it toward him. He spread his hands and tried to grab the oar. The flat end of the long wooden shaft slipped from his wind-struck and rain-soaked hands. Soft mud crept inside his toenails that desperately clutched the shifting ground beneath; his body gave up balance and was just a slant away from plummeting into the darkness of the turbulent river. Boatman Gauri screamed again, "Hey-ho! Watch out, Brother, be on your guard!" And right then, Noor Mohammad grabbed the flat end of the wooden shaft in a strong and sturdy clutch.